A SPIDER IN THE GARDEN

COURTNEY DAVIS

5 Prince Publishing

Copyright © 2022 by Courtney Davis, A SPIDER IN THE GARDEN

All rights reserved.

This is a fictional work. The names, characters, incidents, and locations are solely the concepts and products of the author's imagination, or are used to create a fictitious story and should not be construed as real. No part of this book may be reproduced in any form or by any electronic or mechanical means, including information storage and retrieval systems, without written permission from the author, except for the use of brief quotations in a book review.

Published by 5 PRINCE PUBLISHING & BOOKS, LLC

PO Box 865, Arvada, CO 80001

www.5PrinceBooks.com

ISBN digital: 978-1-63112-276-7

ISBN print: 978-1-63112-277-4

Cover Credit: Artist: Marianne Nowicki

I would never have written one, let alone more than one, novel and been able to pursue publishing in the face of disappointments and rejections if it wasn't for the loving support of my husband. Thank you, Brian, for always making me feel like my time spent writing and all the related work, time and travel, is a worthy endeavor.

ACKNOWLEDGMENTS

Thank you to the team at 5 Prince Publishing for giving my novel a chance, and for supporting my dream of seeing my words in print.

A special and ecstatic thank you to Cate Byers, my amazing editor. You took the time to really understand my story and help me make it the best it could be. Thank you for all your hard work and dedication!

A SPIDER IN THE GARDEN

CHAPTER ONE

Aranha walked through the shadows of the city, same as every night, dressed in ripped up black jeans, a black tank top, and black boots. Her long silver hair was braided down her back and although a passerby might not notice, she had three knives tucked strategically into her outfit. Her black eyes darted around, assessing those she passed, wondering if they had left anything in her web, wondering if she would be seeking them out later. She was vigilant as ever for danger, knowing how quickly the tables could turn, how swiftly she could become the hunted. She knew which parts of the city to avoid and she was a master at hiding when she needed to. She hadn't survived two hundred years alone without learning a few tricks.

She strode into an alley where she often found what she was looking for. A web hung nearly invisible between a broken light and a brick wall. She stepped close and reached up, a small brown spider darted away quickly, heading back to the shadows. She smiled at it.

"Don't worry, little friend," she crooned and it stepped out, peering at her curiously with its many black eyes. "I'm only here for the web."

She swept the thin silk into her palm and watched as it glistened on her skin, she loved this part. Her mind filled with images and words, memories and thoughts. She sifted through them, threw out the mundane, the boring and the happy. She was looking for misery, she was looking for lust and she was looking for the perverse.

She wasn't disappointed.

"You could have told me he just passed by," she scolded the spider and turned.

She saw his face clearly in her mind, it was attached to the memory he'd left on the web. Memories were funny things, a person remembered not only what happened or what they did; they often remembered what they thought they looked like while they did it. Sometimes it was more of a third person experience, not always completely accurate, but she'd had lots of practice sorting out what was real and what was fictional in memories. So not only did Aranha get to see the deed that was done, but the face of the perpetrator as well, or at least a personal approximation of their face. People were terrible judges of their own look most of the time. Luckily, she'd been at this for quite a few years and she was able to reconcile the memory of a face with reality, with sufficient accuracy.

The face she saw this time, she recognized passing only moments before. She moved quickly to follow, sliding through the thin crowds. She formed a web between her fingers, sifting as she went, looking for thoughts from him. Brains were as unique as fingerprints and their patterns were marked on the thoughts the webs caught. Even without a face in it, she could match a thought or memory to a person if she'd already found their fingerprint before.

"Hey baby, you lost?" A boy of maybe twenty called from where he was crouched on a stoop. He was dressed in low slung, baggy jeans and a tight white tank top. His dyed-blond hair was cut short and he had a sly smile on his face. His thoughts drifted into the web; *Sexy thing, I wish she would come sit on my lap. I bet she's a firecracker in the sack. She could handle this dick.* He got up to follow her quick pace. "Hey, I'm talking to you. I can help you. I can get you where you need to be." He gave a dark laugh.

Aranha crushed the web in her hand and spun around, she didn't need him to follow her. "Go home, boy. I'm not interested in your little dick."

"Whoa, you got quite the mouth on you! Sounds like you need someone to teach you some manners." He sauntered closer.

She didn't have time to lure him away and teach him a lesson on respecting women, she had a mission. The fact that he was inhibiting her right now was irritating, but she knew he was harmless. His thoughts had been lecherous, not violent. He thought of himself as a Don Juan and couldn't imagine a woman resisting his advances. Of course, if she were to respond to them, he would likely not know how to take things to the next level. He looked like an idiot and probably lived in his mother's basement while telling people she was just his roommate. She let him stare at her for a moment, taking in her fully black eyes, they never passed for human. Then she opened her mouth and let her long black fangs extend.

That did the trick. She could smell the urine as he pissed his pants, standing frozen to his spot. He wasn't even man enough to run for his life, he'd stand there and let her eat him. "Stupid boy," she hissed and turned, rushing now to try and catch up to the man she'd been tracking.

Aranha spun another web in her hand and sifted once again, irritated that the stupid boy may have ruined her chances. She didn't always succeed in finding the owner of thoughts she decided to pursue, but she rarely failed, and this was a situation she refused to give up on.

She wasn't sure why she was here, but she knew she could do something about the other monsters out there. She'd seen that he had a small boy in his basement, chained up like a goddamn animal! She let the anger fill her and sharpen her senses; this kind of disgusting being didn't deserve to walk the earth. This wasn't someone she could let slip through her web.

Aranha hurried through the streets, passing people who hardly registered her existence. Thoughts flowed through her web and she looked for the pattern she'd felt from the monster she was chasing. As always, she was also watching for scent or thought from any other night creatures. She could never let her guard down, couldn't risk a run in with one of them. A shudder ran through her at the thought of what would happen if she did. She ignored the part of her that wished for it, the release from this loneliness and pain. Death. The end to all of the darkness and filth, the horror that was this place. It could stop... she could stop...

She shook the dark thoughts away and hurried on, more determined than before. A purpose was driving her. As long as she continued to attend to that purpose, she could keep the suicidal thoughts away. Someday she wouldn't be able to stop it, she knew she would present herself to the beasts that could take her down and she would welcome the release. Not today, not as long as there was a helpless soul cowering in chains that she could help.

"Shit," she grumbled as she caught the familiar scent of vampire nearby. She rushed into an alley and shifted, scrambling out of her pile of clothes and up the side of the brick, backing herself into a tiny hole.

She peered out of the darkness, eight unblinking eyes watching for the enemy. A tall woman with long red hair and pale skin, dressed casually in jeans and a t-shirt, stopped at the entrance to the alley. She sniffed the air delicately and peered with narrowed eyes into the darkness. There was nothing to see, just garbage and stray cats. Aranha had hid her clothes and weapons behind a dumpster but if the vampire decided to walk further in to investigate, she might find them, she might find her.

Aranha was confident in her ability to take out a vampire, especially if it was alone, but they rarely were. They tended to travel in pairs, sometimes flanked by werewolf guards. She would have a hell of a time against a group of more than two, it wasn't worth the risk if she could avoid it. One of the only reasons she survived was because they didn't expect to find her, and if they ran across her scent, they were not likely to know what it was they were smelling. Being the last of a presumed extinct species had its benefits.

Another vampire joined the woman, this man was short and round with a deceptively kind face. He put a hand on the woman's back and she motioned to the alley. He turned with a curious eye and sniffed the air.

Death was right there, staring into the alley, eyes searching the walls, the fire escapes, and the roofline. They stood for a long time and Aranha waited. She was on a mission—tonight was not the night to meet her end.

Tomorrow might feel vastly different, perhaps tomorrow she would kneel in front of those two and present her neck, close her eyes and let the final darkness seep into her soul. It would sweep her off this earth and she would find herself in another place, or nowhere at all.

The vampires eventually continued on, but Aranha didn't move for another ten minutes just to be sure. A spider crawled over to investigate who had intruded on her home. They looked at each other and Aranha tapped one of her feet to communicate that she was friendly, and would be leaving soon. The spider was satisfied with that and moved along.

Aranha crawled to the ground and shifted back to human, then dressed as quickly as she could. She headed out to the street, scanning for danger, then turned in the opposite direction that the vampires had gone. She knew she had lost the human for sure now, but she had an idea of where to head. The memory showed a basement, no doubt it was a house and not an apartment because he would need privacy. Since the man was walking, it was likely he lived close and there was only one small neighborhood of houses within reasonable walking distance. She had a destination in mind and set off with determined steps.

The neighborhood street was quiet when she got there, it was quite late and most humans would be settled in for the night. Houses in disrepair lined both sides of the street along with cars in a similar state. It wasn't a nice neighborhood. Maybe it had been once, thirty or more years ago, but now it was a smear of decaying humanity.

She was going to have to get close to the houses one at a time to search properly, she couldn't risk missing the boy. She took a deep breath, resigned to the search, even if it took all night. She would never allow a helpless being to be treated like what she'd seen. Sometimes she wondered if humans didn't deserve their place as food for the supernaturals, the way they treated each other was horrendous.

Aranha started with the first house, moving close, sticking to shadows. She knew she was looking for someone in a basement, so she concentrated on basement windows. She crouched and peered, holding out a webbed hand to try and catch anything alive down there.

House after house was blank. Even a sleeping brain gives off waves of dreaming she would have caught. The poor thing wasn't in any of those, or... she was too late. She wasn't giving up though, not until she'd checked every basement, so she carried on. Catching the mundane thoughts of humans going about their life, or dreaming of better things. Some were drunk, and raging in their minds about how they could have been great, if only this or if it weren't for that. Humans were always blaming others for their situations, not knowing how easily they could just make a different choice, how it wasn't too late to take themselves out of whatever hell they'd made. Often the only thing holding them back was an addiction; drugs, alcohol, or sex that they refused to give up. Humans too often chose those addictions over their own wellbeing or happiness. Self-destruction seemed to be ingrained in humanity. The drug brains were the worst, just dark pits of despair. They reminded Aranha of her own darkness and the pit she often slipped into where she wanted to seek out an end to all of it. Crawling out of that tar pit was a hell of its own. So far, she didn't regret that she had made the journey over and over, but it never completely left her; as if she always had one foot stuck in the cloying black pit, ready to overtake her if she just let go a little more.

Perhaps these humans felt the same way, maybe it was why so many of them didn't run away when faced with a creature who wanted them for dinner, why their instincts froze them or drew them closer rather than told them to run. They were deep in that pit and their escape was standing in front of them in the form of sharp teeth and claws. Perhaps their predilection to addictions was why humans were prey, not predators. A predator's instinct was survival above all else, a predator would never give themselves over to something that would dull the senses and leave them open to harm, no addiction would get in the way of a predator's desire for what they wanted.

What did all predators want? Prey and power; to be fair, these were probably just other forms of addictions. Things that pulled and prodded the being in one direction or another, kept them from seeing themselves for the harmful beings they were.

Aranha shook herself out of the familiar dark train of thought. She wasn't sure where she fit, she knew she wasn't prey, knew her instincts were for survival, but power wasn't something she desired either. The only thing that came close to being a desire, was purpose, she wanted a purpose and that kept her going out every night in search of those who most deserved their place at the bottom of the food chain. Because she also needed prey to survive, and until she could let herself die, she was forced to survive.

She wasn't instinctually prey; she wasn't fully predator... she was other and that suited her just fine.

As her mind flipped through the meaning of her own existence, and whether or not she deserved to continue it, she kept looking and finally she found something in a small grey house. She bent down to a window that was barred, that was her first clue that this might be the place, none of the other houses had barred basement windows. She pushed her hand close, web strung between each finger. There was a curtain on the inside of the window but a crack told her it was dark in there and as far as she could tell, the whole house was quiet, not a light or noise anywhere within.

She didn't have to wait long; she got a stream of random images. Someone was down there, dreaming, and it wasn't her perpetrator, but it might be his victim. Now she needed to know if it was someone's teenage son, or if it was a prisoner in chains. She straightened and walked around the back of the house, slinking smoothly through the shadows. She tried the back door, locked. She could take care of that easy enough though. She listened carefully at the door for a moment hearing nothing, then picked the lock and slipped inside. She was still sifting for thoughts but she couldn't get anything, if there was someone else in the house, they weren't close.

She slunk through the darkness without issue, her eyes saw well without much light. She'd come into the kitchen from a back porch and spied a door that had a heavy lock on it that was far too excessive for an indoor basement. Excitement filled her, this was definitely a sign she'd found the right place. She didn't want to waste time trying to pick the lock now that she was so sure. With a small bit of effort, she was able to rip the lock off the door, splintering the cheap wood. She froze after the cracking noise reverberated around the house. If someone was asleep upstairs or in the next room, they would have definitely heard that, and she was prepared to fight. She had a hand on a knife and was crouched in an attack ready position, waiting.

She heard a groan in the basement but nothing else. After a moment she went down. She kept the knife ready, in case she was wrong about what she was about to encounter. The smell that hit her mid stairway was intense and she knew the poor boy had been down there for a long time. When she reached the bottom of the steps, she saw him and she had to bite her lip to keep from crying out in rage.

He looked like a pile of rags thrown on a dirty pad on the floor. He was shivering and shaking and she wasn't sure if he was awake or dreaming still; his thought pattern was erratic. She put the knife away after her web caught no other thoughts in the room.

"Can you hear me?" she whispered. "My name is Aranha, and I mean you no harm." She held out her hands to show that they were empty.

"Get out of here, he will come back, he'll take you too," the boy croaked out. He sounded like the words were painful to say and he didn't move from his fetal position as he spoke.

Aranha was vibrating with rage, how could anyone be

treated like this, why were there people on earth who would do such a thing to another, it made no sense! She knelt by him, afraid to touch him, afraid she would hurt him while she tried to help.

"I am going to get those chains off you. I could rip them off but I don't want to harm you, do you know where the key is?" She knew it would be faster to rip them off, but it wouldn't be gentle.

"He keeps it in his pocket."

"Is he here?"

"I don't think you would have gotten this far if he was, Ma'am."

"What's your name?"

"Jonah."

"Okay, Jonah I am going to go see if I can find the key."

"You should get out of the house before he comes back, he's going to be so angry if he knows you were here, he'll—"

"He won't hurt you ever again, and I *will* get you out of here." She touched his head gently and he jerked as if she'd slapped him. "I won't harm you, Jonah, I swear it. No one is going to harm you ever again," she said fiercely. Every instinct in her was crying out to help the boy, tears of anger stung the backs of her eyes and her fangs extended, wanting nothing more than to tear apart the monster who had done this.

"Please, Ma'am, it is better for us both if you get out while you can." He moved his head slightly and she saw he had deep blue eyes in a dirty face, sunken cheeks, and cracked lips.

He looked starved and weak. She wondered when the last time he'd had any water or food was. What would be the point of this torture? Aranha's hands fisted and she must have had a terrifying look on her face because Jonah scrambled away, groaning with every movement.

"He will die this night," she vowed. "I am going up to find a key. If I don't find it, I will be back and I will rip those off you as carefully as I can. I won't leave the house without you." She hoped her words were reassuring but his eyes closed and he just sighed sadly.

As she walked away, she heard him sobbing behind her and she couldn't stop herself from punching the wall as she went up the stairs. This was why she was here, this was why she was on earth, to stop this kind of atrocity from going unpunished. A bit of the darkness lifted from her soul; she had a purpose in this moment.

She started in the kitchen, searching for a key, then found the bedroom upstairs and rummaged through drawers. No luck. She was about to just go rip the chains off him when she heard the front door open. She pulled out a knife and smiled, her fangs descended and she waited. She would have been upset to miss out on the punishment part of this rescue mission. She would have come back the next night for it if she'd had to, but waiting was always so frustrating.

The man didn't turn on any lights as he fumbled through the house, he was likely drunk, and on his way to abuse Jonah. Aranha crept out of the bedroom and down the stairs. She was fast and stealthy; the human wouldn't detect her until it was too late. She was in the kitchen doorway when he got to the now ripped open basement door. He was staring at it, dumbfounded, weaving slightly; definitely drunk.

"What the hell?" he slurred.

"Sorry, I didn't have a key," she said casually.

He spun around and faced her with surprise that turned quickly to lustful hope. "Well, hello there, is it Christmas? You look like an angel wrapped in a bow."

"I am your death, dear. You've been a very bad boy." She held her voice steady, conversational, as she spoke to him.

His face slowly registered surprise then turned angry. "Get out of my house, bitch. My son is no concern of yours."

"Your son? This is how you treat your son?" She spoke carefully, trying to keep from lashing out immediately.

"He's not what you think, he's an animal!"

"The only animal I see here is you." She stepped forward and he stepped back, moonlight slid in through a window and she knew he must be finally registering the inhuman blackness of her eyes. She smiled, letting him see her fangs.

"You're one of them!" he gasped.

"No one else on earth is like me, but there are far too many like you," she said simply and shoved him down the stairs.

He tumbled and rolled, in his drunken stupor he was unable to steady himself and he landed with a satisfying thud at the bottom. He groaned but didn't get up. She was a little disappointed as she walked down the stairs. He deserved torture, but he obviously wasn't going to stay conscious long enough for much of it.

"Where's the key?" she hissed.

"Fuck you," he groaned.

She let her black fangs out, dripping venom on his face as she hissed. His eyes widened with fear and he clutched his chest, his body convulsed, he gasped for air, and his eyes rolled back in his head as his heart beat erratically then stopped.

"Shit... that was disappointing," she sighed. "Not going to waste a meal though."

She turned to look at Jonah, he was crouching now, looking at her with fear and shock.

"Don't watch," she said and turned back to the disgusting man on the floor. She bit into his neck and filled him with enough venom to liquefy his insides in a matter of days. Then she shoved him out of the way. No need to wrap him in a web, he was already dead.

CHAPTER TWO

She stepped back and looked down at the dead man, feeling satisfied that she'd helped rid the world of one more disgusting piece of trash. In a few days she'd come back and drink what was left of his insides. She dug around his pockets and found the key to the chains. She took a deep breath and made sure her fangs were retracted and her face clear of any blood or venom before she turned to the now quivering boy.

"Vampire?" he croaked as she walked slowly forward.

"No, I am much cooler and much more rare." She gave him a wink, hoping to relax his nerves.

"I'm a werewolf," he said simply, and she froze as she was about to unlock him.

He was her enemy; she'd just saved one of the only creatures on the planet that could kill her. She looked into his frightened face, he was a young man, maybe nineteen or twenty when he'd been turned, and he was scared. Who knew how long he'd been here? He was nearly starved to death. Tortured by his own father! Parents were supposed to protect their children! "Fuck," she hissed and undid his chains. They burned her skin, unsurprisingly silver, the old man knew what he was doing.

"Thank you," he croaked.

"I am going to take you somewhere safe, then we will figure out what to do."

"He's—" Jonah croaked.

"Yeah, dead. He can't hurt you anymore. Now don't bite me, okay? I'm not going to harm you."

He looked horrified by the idea and she smiled.

"Werewolves don't usually like my kind," she explained.

"You're the most beautiful thing I've ever seen in my entire life," he whispered, then looked embarrassed.

"Can you walk?"

"I—I don't know. I haven't eaten in days," he sounded ashamed and she saw tears start to fall on his cheeks again.

She wanted to kill the bastard all over again for treating this poor creature this way. Enemy or not, he didn't deserve this treatment. "Don't worry, I'm stronger than I look." She reached down and scooped him up. He whined and shivered but he didn't pull away and he didn't tell her to put him down. She took that as consent and left the house. "You'll never have to come back here," she promised.

Aranha cursed herself the entire time she carried the boy to her apartment. She did everything she could to avoid these dangerous creatures, but there was no way she could have left him there, he never would have survived on his own. He could hardly move he was so malnourished, and his spirit was undoubtedly just as damaged as his body. He would have died there alone or gone crazed and killed some people, neither was acceptable to her. She wasn't sure this was the right choice either, but she knew it was better than the other options currently open.

She had so many questions; how long had he been locked up there, when and how had he been turned, and why wasn't he in a pack? It was highly unusual for a werewolf to turn someone and leave them on their own, it was dangerous. His father obviously hadn't been one or he never would have gotten so spooked by Aranha and he'd have been a better fighter. He had known what Jonah was, otherwise he never would have used chains of pure silver. Sometimes human folklore was just right enough to make them dangerous.

She didn't speak to him as she walked, just held him tightly. Anyone who saw them would probably think she was carrying a bundle of clothes, he was so small and frail. She stuck to shadows anyway, it was her usual habit to keep from sight. When they got to her small apartment, she hurried in then shut and locked the door behind them. He was asleep as she laid him gently on her bed.

Aranha looked down at the boy, he smelled terrible and looked half dead. "What am I going to do with you?" she whispered with a shake of her head.

Jonah whined and trembled in his sleep. She pulled a blanket up to cover him and turned on a small lamp in the corner. Her room was sparse, she didn't keep much because she moved so often, it wasn't safe for her to stay long anywhere. The bedroom consisted of a mattress on the floor, a dresser with a lamp and piles of clothes and weapons everywhere. At least it wasn't a drafty basement and there were no chains, he should be comfortable and if he didn't freak out, he should be safe.

She imagined he would sleep a while and need food when he woke up. She didn't keep food in the house because she didn't eat it, didn't have guests over who ate it, well, didn't have guests over. She grabbed some cash from her stash and left the apartment on a new mission. There was a gas station not far from there and she would be able to pick up a few things. When he woke up, she would find out what he liked and go out for more food and other supplies he'd need, like clothes. She couldn't help laughing at the thought of going grocery shopping, that was one experience she'd never had in her long life.

She wasn't sure what he might eat, but assumed meat was a good choice. She bought all the jerky they had and some various bags of chips and bottles of juice. She was wearing sunglasses to keep her eyes hidden from the checker who looked at her like she was about to rob the place. She smiled as sweetly as she could manage to try and settle his nerves.

"Nice night," she said conversationally.

"Yeah, dark out there," he said, pointedly looking at her glasses.

She just smiled and paid, then hurried out. She was anxious to get back, worried her houseguest would wake up scared and try to leave, no doubt harming himself along the way. She still wasn't sure that she hadn't made a huge mistake, but then, she also wasn't sure that this wasn't fate. There was so much chance involved with what she caught in a web. The chance that she'd even gotten a clear picture of him when his father had passed by was a one in a million. Her heart ached remembering seeing him there, what he must have gone through and how much he didn't deserve to be treated like that; no one did. Her steps quickened and by the end she was nearly running to her door, she had to make sure he was still there, that he was still okay. If he ran off, she may never be able to find him and if another werewolf or vampire found him first, they'd likely kill him rather than deal with him.

She was filled with a strange and unexpected relief when she found him still laying in a ball in the middle of her bed. She set the bags beside the mattress and sat in front of the closed bedroom door watching him sleep. He was her enemy, but he was just an innocent boy. She couldn't merge the two in her mind and it irritated her.

She fell asleep there and woke with a fright, she jumped to

her feet, knife drawn. Her mind swam in grogginess as she tried to figure out why she'd been sitting up sleeping.

"Please, I'm sorry, I'm sorry," Jonah cried and moaned, cowering from her and dropping a bottle of juice to spill all over the floor.

"Fuck," she whispered as she remembered the night before.

"I—I thought it was for me. I'm so hungry, I'm so sorry. Please don't hurt me, I'll do better, I'll—I'll do anything you want." His voice caught and she knew tears were not far behind.

"Stop it," she hissed. She couldn't stand his cowering from her.

He froze and tears streaked down his cheeks, making clean lines in the grime.

Aranha sighed heavily and picked up the juice, now mostly empty, and handed it to him. He took it with shaking hands, eyeing her cautiously. "It's all for you, I just don't wake up well," she grumbled and went to fetch a towel for the mess.

When she came back, he was shoving an entire bag of jerky into his mouth. She smiled at him when he froze again. "It's all for you, I don't eat."

He eyed her cautiously. "What are you?" he asked with a mouth full of jerky.

She wasn't sure how much she should tell him. "Eat, shower, then we'll talk."

He looked wary but he ate, greedily, and she wondered if he was going to choke. She studied him as he ate. Shaggy, light brown hair, bright blue eyes. Every inch of skin she saw was covered in bruises, dirt and scrapes. She wished she could go back and kill that bastard nice and slow.

She hissed at her own thoughts and he froze, whimpering. "Ma'am?" he whispered.

She retracted her fangs and smiled. "Sorry, just thinking. Don't worry Jonah, you're safe here."

He didn't look like he believed her. "How did you find me?"

"I followed the clues in his thoughts." She didn't dare call him his father, and she didn't know his name. He didn't deserve recognition anyway, he was a monster.

"Oh..." Jonah ate slower, contemplating. "You're not a vampire?"

"No."

"You're not a werewolf?"

"No."

"But you aren't human, and the chains burned you like they did me."

"Yes."

"I'm safe?" he asked carefully. "I—I can do things for you... whatever it is you want, I can do it."

"You don't need to do anything; I don't want anything from you. I just couldn't stand to let you suffer. No one deserves that." She spoke as calmly as she could, but anger seeped into her voice. "Yes, you are safe." She smiled and started cleaning up the garbage. "Now how about a shower? I think I have some clothes you can wear until we can get something more appropriate."

He winced as he moved off the mattress, but he managed it and shuffled after her. She showed him where he could find what he needed in the bathroom. "Use this ointment on open wounds. You should heal quickly now that you have some food in you, but some of those look deep. When you're in the shower I will come grab your dirty clothes and throw them out. I'll leave something for you to put on when you get out."

"Thank you, Ma'am."

"Aranha."

"That's a weird name," he said, then immediately cowered as if she were going to strike him for saying it.

"Yep, it is," she said simply and left. She had to take deep breaths on the other side of the door. Everything about that boy was tearing at her heart. She'd never thought of herself as a nurturer, never desired children or even the responsibility of a pet. The desire to help and shield this boy was something so unexpected it scared her a little. Was it just because she was so desperate for a reason to live, something to justify her life? She wasn't sure that saving a werewolf was validation for continuing her own immortal existence as a killer.

When she heard the water running, she knocked and stepped in when he called.

"I'm leaving clothes on the counter."

"Thank you," he said with a sigh, obviously enjoying the warm shower.

Aranha walked out to her living room and sighed with less enjoyment. This place was small and messy. She didn't need to impress anyone, but she felt bad for her small guest. She did her best to clean up a bit, moving piles of mostly clothing. She had a small couch and television on top of a pile of books. She didn't have a kitchen table and her kitchen was empty, she'd need to remedy that. She threw out his clothes as well as what she'd worn yesterday and the bedding he'd been on. His stench was overwhelming and she was sure he hadn't had access to a proper toilet for a while. She opened windows to air out the place and figured it was the best she could do for now.

She sank onto the couch and grumbled. How long did she plan to keep him? How long until he realized they were enemies and decided to rip out her throat? Was this just a backdoor to her own suicide? Bring the killer home and feed it, help it get its strength back so it can cleanly end her?

When he slunk out of the bathroom dressed in a Skid Row t-shirt and baggy sweatpants, she was shocked to see his hair was actually a dirty blond and he had dark eyelashes around those bright blue eyes. He still looked frail and beaten, but he was improving. Not having silver chains on that were draining his body, and some actual food in his belly, had done a lot to aid in his supernatural ability to heal.

He stood there looking unsure, one arm crossed over his body holding the other arm, biting his lip and darting his lowered eyes around. He dipped his head and shuffled a foot. "So, I guess I better go."

"Yeah, where do you think you should go? Because it looks like you better sit down and let me get you something more to eat." She wasn't sure where this motherly instinct was coming from but she wanted nothing more than to wrap him in her arms and rock back and forth cooing into his ear that it was all going to be okay and no one was ever going to hurt him again. She wished she could tell him that the boogeyman wasn't real and there wasn't a monster in the closet, but the best she could do was reassure him that she'd killed the one she'd found and she would tear the head off any other that came near.

He walked slowly over to the couch, still not looking at her. "I don't have anywhere to go, Ma'am, and I don't have a way to repay you with money."

"I don't need anything from you, Jonah, now sit before I pick you up and make you sit."

He hurried to obey, sitting as far from her as possible on the small couch.

"You smell much better," she laughed. "I threw out those old clothes." His face flamed and she immediately felt bad, she shouldn't have said anything to embarrass him. "What kind of food do you like?" she asked quickly to change the subject to more pleasant things.

"Oh, anything is fine."

"Jonah," she said harshly and waited for him to meet her gaze, he only went as far as her chin so she reached out and lifted his until their eyes met. "I am going to take care of you, you owe me nothing. I will only ask two things of you."

Fear filled his eyes and she wondered what horrors he must have been subjected to. It was tempting to use her webs to find out, but she didn't like to use them to invade anyone's privacy.

"Don't tell anyone what I am and don't bite me. Your venom is toxic to me, as mine is to you, so keep that in mind."

He nodded quickly. "Yes, oh yes, Ma'am I would never—I won't—I—I don't even know what you are." He gave a tentative smile and it warmed her heart.

"How about I go shopping and you watch TV, then we'll talk."

"Cereal," he said quickly.

"What?"

"I would love some cereal and milk," he said sheepishly.

"Got it. You need lots of protein too. Werewolves are carnivores." She patted his leg and he jumped. "Please don't leave," she instructed and handed him the remote. "I'm going to lock the door when I leave to make sure you're safe, not to keep you in."

"Yes, thank you Ma'am."

"Aranha," she said, a little exasperated.

"Aranha," he said quietly.

"I shouldn't be long." She left with a nervous knot in her stomach, afraid he wouldn't be there when she returned. Unsure what she was going to do if he was... did she know enough about werewolves to help him, and when was the next full moon? He'd need to be somewhere safe when the moon forced him to shift.

It took her a couple of hours to get everything she thought she needed. When she stumbled back into the apartment loaded down with shopping bags, she was exhausted and irritated.

Humans were not her favorite and she'd just had to deal with far too many of them.

"I got cereal," she said proudly as she nearly fell into the room.

Jonah was crouched behind the couch, peering over it like he was expecting a swat team to descend with guns drawn.

"It's just me, can you shut the door please?"

Jonah hurried to do as she asked. "You came back," he said quietly.

"Of course I came back. What did you think?"

"I—I don't know, I just— I just didn't think you would come back," he admitted solemnly.

Fuck, ran through her head as she realized she'd already made a big mistake. Werewolves—new baby werewolves—imprinted on the first one that cared for them after their initial change. Obviously, the abusive father wasn't filling that role, and when she'd stepped in and taken him out of danger, she'd become his mother wolf. Whether she liked it or not, she had a new son, a werewolf son.

"I came back, I live here," she said a little too harshly. Jonah sat on the floor and scooted back away from her. She rolled her eyes and took a breath, then turned and looked at him with as much kindness and compassion as she could manage. "Jonah, come see what I bought you."

He crawled forward slowly. He sat at her feet and laid his head against her leg. "Thank you," he said quietly.

"You haven't even seen what I got."

"Thank you for taking me away. Thank you for coming back."

Aranha reached down and petted his head. "I'll always come back, Jonah, you're mine now." There was no way around it. She wasn't going to let this poor thing out into the world and he wasn't going to leave willingly, at least not yet. So for now, he was hers and she would do everything she could to take care of him.

He pressed his nose against her leg and smelled her. "Yours." She could practically see the werewolf instincts turning in his head, solidifying the bond he was making. At least she could assume he'd never harm her, and he would likely die trying to protect her.

When he was ready, she showed him the food and clothing she'd picked up and promised to take him with her next time so he could pick stuff out for himself. As much for him as for her, trying to decide on a box of cereal on an aisle with a thousand options and screaming children... she'd almost lost her mind.

He, of course, was thankful for everything and had no complaints. He poured a bowl of cereal and settled happily back on the couch. She put away the rest of the stuff, thankful she'd kept the refrigerator plugged in even though she'd never had a use for it. "I don't know how to cook, so hopefully you do."

"I can cook," he said around a mouthful of cereal. "You don't eat?"

"I eat, after my kill has sat for a few days, I drain it." She spoke matter-of-factly. If they were going to be a family of sorts, he was going to have to just accept what she was.

"Like a spider?"

She laughed, "Exactly like a spider."

"Oh! Webmaker, now I get it."

"I'm a shifter like you, except I only shift at will, the full moon won't force me to shift. I can be any type or size of spider. The only thing I can't change is my coloring, always black and silver."

"I only shifted once," he said sadly, staring into his bowl. "I had been out camping with some friends and we were attacked by wolves, werewolves I guess. The funny thing was, there wasn't even a full moon!" he shrugged. "I guess that sort of thing doesn't really matter, werewolves can change any time they want maybe." He looked at Aranha for confirmation.

She nodded. "My understanding is that they can, yes, at will or when angered."

"I was the only survivor, barely made it out. I killed one on my way to the truck, I had a large hunting knife with me and managed to get him in the neck." He paused for a minute and looked thoughtful. "I suppose it may not have killed him, but it stopped him long enough for me to get away. I drove back to town, injured and running a high fever, my father refused to take me to the hospital, said we couldn't afford the bill. So I laid in bed recovering for a few days, super high fever and so much pain. Then after about a week, in the middle of the night it just happened, I changed and it hurt so badly I wished I was dead, begged for death! My dad freaked out and shot me mid-change, almost killed me, I think. When I woke up I was chained."

"The silver would keep you from changing again, even during a full moon. When was that?" Aranha asked quietly. She sat next to him and put a comforting arm around his shoulders.

"Six months or more, I think." He laid his head on her shoulder accepting her comfort. "He—he brought friends home sometimes when he was drunk. Sometimes they were... interested in me," his voice broke and he sobbed deeply, tears pouring out of him.

Aranha pulled him onto her lap and let him cry. No one should have to go through what he'd been through.

When he stopped crying, he extricated himself from her lap looking a bit embarrassed.

"You are safe now, remember that. You'll be strong soon and able to take very good care of yourself."

"And you! I will take care of you, too," he said proudly.

"I'm pretty good at taking care of myself."

His face fell and she regretted her words. "I will be useful, I promise."

"Just be, don't worry about anything else. You are going to have to learn about how to be a werewolf safely. You know about vampires?"

"I was just guessing, if there are werewolves then there have to be vampires, right?"

Aranha laughed at his reasoning, no doubt based on bad movie representations. "Yeah, I guess so."

"And there's, webmakers, that's your kind?"

"One and only, we were killed off."

"By who?" Jonah's level of disbelief and offense was heartwarming.

"Werewolves and vampires actually, which is why it's so important you don't tell them about me. No one can know I exist or I'm afraid they will come after me and if they start expecting to find me, they may be more interested when they catch a bit of my scent."

"Why?"

"Because I pose a danger to them, my venom quickly kills them, as theirs would me."

"And you're the only one? I will keep your secret forever," he vowed. His eyes wide and his tone reverent.

She couldn't help laughing a little to lighten the mood. "Forever is a long time. How old are you?"

"Nineteen. Will I live forever? Will I be forever a scrawny nineteen-year-old?" He looked down at himself and frowned.

"I don't know for sure. I don't know a lot about werewolves, honestly. So, we'll learn together." She couldn't believe those words were coming out of her mouth, and she had no idea how they were going to learn, but they would. She figured she knew enough of the lore to keep him alive and the rest would be a bit of trial and error.

CHAPTER THREE

Aranha strapped on her knives and glanced in the mirror. She looked ready to kick ass.

"You look like a nightmare on steroids," Jonah said from the doorway.

As usual he was munching on something. He'd become quite efficient in the kitchen in the last year and had filled out his body slightly. She was pretty sure he'd never be a large-bodied werewolf, but he was muscular and a bit taller than when she'd found him. It could be that he was just finally standing straight.

He was now fully in control of his werewolf and ran on full moon nights with joy. The trauma he'd endured at his father's hands had left him deeply scarred, he trusted no one but her, and he rarely left her side. They slept on separate mattresses in the same room, though he often crawled into hers and she woke with him cuddled next to her. They spent their days together, avoiding interaction with others for everyone's safety. He was like a puppy following her around unless she told him sternly to stay. It was working out better than she could have expected.

"Good, I'll need to eat, so I must go hunting. You'll have to entertain yourself tonight."

"Shouldn't I join you, watch your back?"

"No, you should stay here and watch TV, read a book maybe. Or perhaps go outside and find a cute girl to waste your time with."

"No thanks, I'll wait for you here."

Like a dog, she sighed. She really wanted him to want to leave the nest, or den rather, at some point, but she wasn't sure that was ever going to happen.

"I think I'll dye my hair," he said, casually running his fingers through the now shoulder length mass of dyed blond hair.

"Yeah, not blond enough?"

"I picked up some blue, thought a change might be good."

"Sounds great." She kissed his cheek and left. She heard a slight whine as the door shut. He was a needy creature, but she loved him.

She waltzed through the streets as invisibly as she could, heading for the webs she'd left. The first couple were empty of anything intriguing but the third was a hit. She saw a memory left by a man who was definitely on the list of deservedly edible humans. She smiled as she locked onto the print of the memory so she could easily find it again. She watched and re-watched; looking for clues as to where he might be heading with this evil intent.

She started back down the street, web between her fingers sifting for the same thought pattern in case she got lucky and he was close by. She'd seen where he was likely going, where he often went and met up with drunk women. Women he could easily victimize. A cheap bar on a street corner, like so many others in New York, it wasn't special, but she had a feeling he was a regular there.

She didn't find him or any sign of his mind as she made her way through the busy streets, but she came to a neon sign proclaiming *Cold Beer* soon enough. This felt like the place he'd been thinking about. Trouble was, she couldn't be certain if he was planning to come here tonight. She was certain this was his regular haunt she'd seen in the disturbing memory, but it wasn't an intention, only a remembrance. Of course, if he followed the pattern of most psychotic abusers, he wouldn't miss a Saturday night out and there had been a feeling of longing in the memory. It made her think he wasn't just remembering the act, but craving the repeating of it. It was enough for her to go on. She stared from across the street a moment, wondering if she could just wait outside and catch the thoughts of any who left, but that could take all night and she hated to leave Jonah alone that long.

This neighborhood wasn't completely without possibility of trouble for her either, and she didn't really want to stay too long if she could help it. If she went in, she would have to deal with getting hit on, and that always put her in a sour mood. Not that she didn't appreciate a male body every now and then, it was just that humans rarely survived the experience and she hated to kill someone if they didn't really deserve it.

With a determined mind, she strode into the dark establishment, hoping her serious face would keep most suitors at bay. She gained a lot of looks as she made her way to the bar, but none made a move to approach, that was good. She tested the air carefully, as she always did when she entered a building. She was looking for traces of werewolves and vampires. She got nothing and she relaxed the slightest bit. There *was* something odd about the smell here, but she brushed it off, there were a lot of humans and alcohols here, their mixed smells were a lot to take in and sort through.

The place was decorated with old sports memorabilia, nothing surprising there. She figured the owner probably was a hell of a ball player in high school and couldn't let go of those days when he had been satisfied with his life. Probably hated everything about his life now. Humans were terrible about living in the past, they wasted so much of their short lives looking the wrong way.

The stool she slid onto was wooden and worn down from thousands of patrons drinking their troubles away. Sometimes she envied human's ability to forget their troubles in a glass. Alcohol didn't affect her, she wasn't sure why, but she knew she could drink as much as she wanted and never get that blissful peace that humans so often sought.

Aranha slipped a hand under the bar and laid a web there between the underside of the bar and a patch of skin revealed by the strategic rips in her jeans. As long as she had skin contact, she would have a direct line to stray thoughts and memories in the place. If he was here or walked in, she was sure to sense it. Then she would lure and strike, and he wouldn't be able to ever hurt anyone else. Her heart beat a little faster in anticipation of ridding the world of another killer, it was her main purpose for existing, she was sure.

The crowd was as she'd come to expect in places like this; barflies of the male and female type, looking more than halfway to drunk even though it was early into the evening, and some rowdy bachelors and bachelorettes who would likely find their way to each other before the night ended. The pool tables were full and the jukebox was playing something from the eighties that she wasn't sure she recognized.

"What can I get you?"

"Blue Moon," she answered without thinking, not turning from scanning the crowd. Thoughts and memories were flowing freely, but none matched the print of her perpetrator. Maybe he hadn't come in, maybe it had only been a passing thought, or a fleeting memory. Maybe she'd gotten this one wrong... but she'd been so sure, the memory had been strong and vivid. In her experience, anyone thinking that hard about an evil deed, was committed to going through with it. It didn't eliminate incidentals like he got hit by a bus on the way here or arrested for whacking off in an alley. Those were long shots though, most people were creatures of habit and his habit was dark.

"You haven't been in before," the bartender said as he slid her glass across the bar.

With a sigh of annoyance, she turned to him and picked up the glass. He caught her full attention immediately and she sucked in a breath. He was over six feet tall, muscles bulging in his half-buttoned plaid shirt with rolled up sleeves. Blue eyes looked out of a tan face and his long blond hair was French braided down his back and shaved up the sides. He was gorgeous and definitely her type, but that wasn't the only thing that was making her pause, attraction wasn't filling her with terror and making her want to turn and run as far and as fast as she could.

"What are you?" Aranha asked, breathless. He wasn't human and he wasn't a vampire or werewolf—this was something she'd never encountered—his scent was sweet and tempting, not frightening. This was the confusing scent she'd gotten a whiff of when she'd entered the place. She didn't trust it, or him. She debated making a run for it right then. This was it for her in this city, she needed to disappear. Central America crossed her mind. Jonah would probably like a change of scenery, some place without all the bad memories.

He smiled and leaned forward, placing one arm on the bar between them, his face mere inches from hers. She couldn't move. His breath was minty and she couldn't help licking her lips as her eyes settled on his mouth.

"I'm Dag, and I am a daywalker. You are a webmaker and I

don't appreciate you sifting the thoughts of my paying customers."

Aranha moved back and narrowed her eyes at the man. His skin was sun-kissed, his lips delicious and kissable, he even smelled like a sunny summer day. Of course he was a daywalker; a blood drinker who had the ability to withstand the light of the sun. "I thought you were extinct," she said quietly. She'd never met one, but she didn't doubt his words.

"If I was extinct, I wouldn't be slinging beer in the depths of New York. Why are *you* here and why do you smell like werewolf?"

"I tracked a killer to your establishment; I intend to intercept him before he removes another innocent life from the planet." She ignored the werewolf remark, she would protect Jonah at all costs.

He looked unconvinced. "You some kind of savior to these lowly humans?" He raised one eyebrow in a devilishly enticing way.

"They deserve to live as much as us, maybe more..." she mumbled. "I have to eat, and the way I see it, if I take out a dirt bag instead of an innocent, then great."

Dag stood up and looked around the bar. "I doubt any of these drunks or partygoers are who you're looking for."

"I saw this place in his mind. He's hunted here before." She watched Dag's eyes widen then narrow, he obviously didn't like the idea of someone hunting in his territory. "I will remove the pest once he arrives, don't worry," she assured him.

"A spider catching barflies?" he said with a laugh.

"Only the killer kind."

"Well, you will do nothing without my permission, this is my business, and these are my patrons."

"You would allow a killer to live? To prove what point?" she challenged.

"Beer! Barkeep! Another round here," a drunk voice shouted from a table.

"Better take care of your *patrons*," Aranha sneered.

"Don't move," he hissed and moved to get the requested beer.

She couldn't take her eyes off him as he moved. His movements were swift and efficient, faster than a human, but nothing compared to what he probably could do. She wondered what kind of man he was in a fight. She could imagine him on a battlefield wielding an ax, or coming at an enemy with his bare hands and fangs bared. He was deadly, she was certain, and she found it extremely attractive. She thought about him and his species, wondering in what other ways they differed from vampires. Daywalkers... Her mother had told her very little about them, had made them seem ancient and extinct, much like webmakers. Maybe Dag was the last of his kind, maybe he was as alone in this world as she was.

She stopped that line of thinking. It would not get her anywhere she needed to be. One orphan hanging around was enough, she didn't need to try and adopt this one, no matter how sexy he was.

He turned and caught her staring, he raised an eyebrow and lifted one side of his lips in a half smile. She turned away quickly, drinking her beer and concentrating on the incoming thoughts.

"You read mine and I promise you won't like what you find," he hissed as he passed her with the pitcher of beer.

She couldn't control it, but she didn't tell him that. Thoughts just floated uninhibited; her web caught what it caught. She could direct the web at someone and increase her chances of catching what their mind was throwing out, but even that wasn't a guarantee. Some people's thoughts were very loud, some quiet.

The thoughts she was catching now were not surprising and not what she was looking for. She tuned them out and drank her beer, watching the front door through the mirror at the back of the bar. Her target wasn't here now, but he would be, she was sure.

Fuckable.

The thought floated into her web and she smiled, knowing Dag had thought it as he'd passed her on his way back behind the bar. He busied himself with dishes and serving a few other customers, ignoring her, which she was fine with. She didn't need his interference and she didn't want his attention. When things slowed a bit, he slid her another beer.

"Thanks."

"If you're going to sit there looking like a pissed off dominatrix, you might as well be drinking. I think you've scared at least one of my customers away so far."

"That old guy with the green shirt? He thought I was a prostitute; wanted to approach me but couldn't work up the nerve so he left feeling like a failure." She shrugged. "I think it was the best option."

Dag laughed and Aranha was startled by the delightful sound. His mouth was wide and she could see his fangs tucked away in there, a human wouldn't notice them until they extended fully, then it would be too late.

"Poor old Darren, he's got a wife at home, so I bet he feels pretty terrible for even thinking about it."

"A wife?" Aranha frowned, she hadn't caught anything in his thoughts about her. "Are you sure?"

"Talks about her all the time, name's Teresa."

Aranha sifted back through the thoughts she'd recently caught, found the one that had caught her attention from Darren. It had been loud and directed at her, she couldn't ignore it. Having the signature of his thought, she was able to sift through the others and quickly identify his others without a problem. He'd lusted after almost every female in the place, he'd grumbled about the price of the beer and he had envied Dag's physique. Nothing about a wife. "Well, if he does have a wife, he wasn't thinking about her tonight."

"I suppose he doesn't come in here to drink too much and remember his life." Dag shrugged. "Still no sign of your victim?"

"Not a victim, perpetrator. You are the one who looks for victims, daywalker."

"Ha! I haven't killed someone in a very long time," he whispered, leaning toward her over the bar, "and even then, it was always deserved. When's the last time you had blood on your hands?" he challenged.

"I only kill those who deserve to die, and I eat what I kill. It's like hunting and it's always serial killer season." She gave him a playful wink. "Every good spider takes out the pests around them. It's the natural order of things."

"They also tend to eat their mates, is that your habit?" he asked in a husky whisper.

"Wouldn't you like to know," she said saucily.

"Dude! That bitch is huge! Someone call the exterminator," a voice called from across the room and had both Dag and Aranha running toward it.

"Touch it and die," she said when she came to the scene.

A man in his fifties with a belly that showed he drank more beer than anything else, had his shoe in his hand and poised to come crashing down on a delicate black spider about the size of a half dollar.

"Why, is it poisonous? Shit Dag, this place is a dive but I didn't think it was infested." His arm moved, the shoe was descending and the spider wasn't moving; it huddled in a corner and Aranha could feel its paralyzing fear.

She reached for the knife at her back at the same time Dag

reached out inhumanly fast to grab the man's arm, stopping his shoe inches from the frightened spider. Aranha sheathed her knife and picked up the spider, hurrying outside to free her. She couldn't help feeling a kinship for all the arachnids on earth, she spent a fair amount of time as one of them.

"What were you doing in there?" she chastised the spider as she set it safely in an alley. It looked up at her thankfully and an image entered her mind of cool air and pressing heat. The spider had been appreciating the air conditioning inside the bar.

"Is it okay?" Dag asked as she stood up and watched the spider scurry away.

"She was just looking for a cool place to build a web." Aranha turned and came nose to nose with Dag, he was tall, but so was she.

"I would have let him smash it if you weren't about to stab him for it," he stated simply.

"I know," she replied with deadly calm.

"And you don't see a problem with stabbing him for smashing the thing?"

"The *thing* has a life that's worth as much as yours and mine. Maybe more than humans, they tend to be vicious creatures who kill without thought."

"Unlike you?" he challenged.

"Unlike me," she said between clenched teeth.

His eyes locked onto her mouth, and she couldn't help flicking her tongue out and running it over her lips—it was her nature to entice a mate, draw him in, and eat him when she was done with him. She spun a web between her fingers but before she could catch his thoughts, he grabbed her hand and swiped it off.

"I said, *don't* try to read my thoughts, *webmaker*," he hissed.

Aranha pulled away, ready to fight. "Don't flatter yourself. Someone just walked into your bar, I was checking to see if it was my perpetrator," she lied. Someone *had* entered the bar, but it hadn't crossed her mind to worry about it in that moment.

"Well, let's go check him out, shall we? But if you try to pull a knife in my bar again, I will have to remove you. Permanently. I try very hard to keep blood from spilling in my establishment."

"Because you would go into a craze and kill everyone in sight without a thought?" she shot back.

"I have more self-control than you, obviously," he said calmly, and went inside without waiting for her or holding the door.

"You'd rip out a man's throat if he were about to smash a child with his car. Innocent life is to be protected," she said to no one.

She took a steadying breath before walking in. Being around him was jarring to her nerves in a way she wasn't used to. She'd been threatened many times in her long life, she'd felt lust, and she'd felt hate. He was like all of that wrapped up in a package that made her mouth water and her fangs descend. He also distracted her from her mission, and she didn't like that at all.

When she walked back inside, Dag was behind the bar serving drinks to a group of bachelorettes. The man who'd almost received a knife in the arm was drinking happily, and the new arrival was in a corner, trying to get the attention of the lone waitress. Aranha was wasting no time; she walked over and asked if she could join the man. He happily agreed. She quickly spun a web and caught his thoughts as he talked about his profitable furniture business, he hadn't even asked her name. His thoughts revealed exactly what she expected from such a narcissist.

Images of a dark room, a dirty mattress and blood, so much blood.

"Hey, this waitress is taking forever, you wanna get out of here?" she asked brightly.

He froze mid-sentence, stuttered agreement, then grabbed his coat and stood. "I know just the place," he said with a grin. His thoughts were elated, this was easier than he'd expected, easier than usual. He thought she was probably a whore and he was definitely doing the world a favor by ridding it of her.

She smiled back; her thoughts were nearly identical. The difference was, she *knew* she was ridding the world of a worthless being, he only told himself that to make himself feel better about indulging his dark desires. She followed him out, turning her head at the door to meet Dag's eyes, and just to be sure she was pissing him off, she reached up and slapped a web up above the door on her way out.

CHAPTER FOUR

Dag stalked over to the door and whipped a rag at the offending web. He couldn't believe she'd walked into his bar, couldn't believe she even existed! It had been at least two hundred years since he'd heard of a living webmaker; three since he'd seen one with his own eyes, his mother. She'd left the clan to try and convince a coven of webmakers to join them for safety, she'd not returned, but word from a pack of werewolves did come. The wolves had taken out the threat of the entire coven including his mother.

He'd known what the woman was immediately. She smelled like morning dew caught on a spider's web mixed with that little bit of magic he knew meant she wasn't human, she was something like him. It had helped that she'd had a spider web clinging to the leg of her pants when she'd walked in; he'd put it all together before she'd even sat down and ordered a beer, never even looking at him. He'd been able to study her fully before she'd noticed him. Her silvery grey hair was intriguing enough, but add to that her black eyes and he wondered how anyone didn't know just by looking at her that she wasn't a human.

Of course, she was very good at keeping her eyes down and she had a pair of sunglasses hanging on her shirt. She probably wore them often, even at night and inside. She was tall, almost as tall as him and her body was slender. She moved with a grace that begged to be watched, and he had, feeling his body react instinctively. When she'd reached for the beer, he'd spotted a small black spider tattooed on her wrist, another tattoo poked out on her back at her shoulders. He couldn't be sure what it was, but it seemed to stretch across her entire back and he wanted desperately to know where it ended.

A glass broke in his grip as his body reacted to the direction his thoughts were heading.

"Whoa, boss! You okay?" Felicity, his waitress, asked as she arrived at the bar with a tray full of empty glasses.

"Yeah, fine. Hey did you recognize that guy who just left with that woman?"

"Frank? He's in here at least once a week, always in the back corner, always creeping on the young drunk girls. How did you not know that?"

Because he was an asshole who didn't serve beers outside of the bar top often, Dag thought. He didn't venture back to the corners of the bar when patrons were there. "Oh yeah." He mumbled as he swept up the mess he'd made. "It's slow, I'm going to make a phone call in my office."

"Okay," she huffed with annoyance and walked around to pour beers herself.

Dag shut himself in his office and paced, unsure what to do. He told himself that he needed to know more about her before he could figure out what the best move was. Was she the last of her kind or were there more? Did she kill indiscriminately like he'd heard some of her kind had? Did she harness the thoughts of others and turn them into dark insidious dreams that haunted her victims? He knew that last one was a stretch, he'd never heard any credible stories about webmakers doing that, but being able to read thoughts of others was undoubtedly a powerful weapon.

Was she one of the good ones? That was the big question. Was she really only interested in killing those who deserve it? Did she live alone and scared? Did her tattoo go all the way down to the sweet curve of her ass? He didn't even know her goddamn name! He bit back a roar and slammed a hand into his desk, hearing the wood crack.

He dropped into his office chair. He had no idea what his true motivation was, but either way, he had to go after her. If he never saw her again... he *would* see her again, and have every one of his questions answered, too. He had to find her before anyone else did, that was for certain. The very fact that she existed put her in danger. She'd smelled like werewolf so she must have had a recent run in. Judging by her still being alive, she must have killed it, that could be cause for alarm amongst the vampires and werewolves. She couldn't have been in the city very long going unnoticed and he doubted she stayed in any one place long. What a lonely life that must be. His heart tightened at the thought of her suffering. He could offer her protection, he *should* offer her protection! She could mean *everything* to their kinds.

He rushed out of his office. "Bar's closed, everybody out!"

Shouts of disagreement and bewilderment went up around him, but he ignored them all.

"What's going on?" Felicity hurried over with somebody's full beer on her tray.

"No charge for the drinks that haven't been paid for, get them all out and lock the doors. I have to go, emergency at my building." He left Felicity standing there with her jaw dropped and the customers settling back down, they heard free beer and they were satisfied, at least for the moment.

As soon as he was outside, he picked up her scent and followed it at a quick pace. Every instinct was screaming; get to her, *now!*

Aranha had no trouble convincing the man, Frank, to go to her apartment. At least that's where she told him they were headed. She led him to one of her many places around the city that she knew was safe for a meal. An empty basement where she could interrogate and punish, then leave him for a few days to liquefy.

Frank had his dirty hand on her back and his beer breath invaded her nostrils as he droned on and on, vacillating between how beautiful she was and how successful and thereby powerful, *he* was. She smiled and nodded at the appropriate times, but didn't bother with conversation, he didn't care what she had to say. His thoughts were running through various scenarios he wanted to put her through and he didn't even notice she barely responded to his vocal dribble.

She pulled him into an alley and down a staircase that led to the basement of an abandoned brick building. He didn't even flinch. In his mind, this was as good a place as any to do to her what he had planned. Even better because it had no connection to him, unlike his own basement. As she wrestled with the locked door, his hands roamed her backside and it took every ounce of control she had, to not lash out at him right then. She stifled a hiss and managed a forced giggle as she got the door open.

"Come on in, have a seat right over there and I'll give you a show." The large open room held a single chair, a bare lightbulb hanging from the ceiling and nothing else. It was completely non-threatening. No chains, no tools of torture; she didn't need any of that, she *was* that.

"Oh yeah, yeah, sure. Just do your thing, I'll pay good money, I promise." His eyes were wide and shifting around the room. He kept wiping his sweaty palms on his pant legs and there was a bubble of spittle at the corner of his thin lips. He was a disgusting human, inside and out, and she wouldn't feel one bit of sorrow over disposing of him.

He sat as she'd instructed and she strutted toward him. She began a dance she'd done more times than she could count. She started at his chest, touching it lightly she walked around him, dragging a thread of web. He didn't even notice, they never did, not until it was too late. This wasn't like the webs she spun for catching thoughts, this was stronger, thicker, and stickier. Once around and he couldn't lift his arms. She stood back as he realized something out of the ordinary was happening.

"What the hell?" he yelled, and shook his body, finding that his arms were pinned in place. He tried to stand but she just pushed him right back down onto the chair. His hand managed to shoot into his pocket where she knew he kept a small knife.

She whipped around him quickly, leaving web around his legs and body, enough that he wasn't able to even attempt standing again, let alone pull out and wield a knife.

"You've been a bad boy, Frank, a very bad boy and I don't think a human like you deserves to continue to prey upon the weak." She laughed and let her fangs slip out slightly. "You *are* the weak, you are *my* prey now."

"Listen lady, I don't know what you think you're doing, but I am not into this sort of thing. I'm not paying you for dominatrix shit."

He probably saw himself as a top predator and couldn't fathom a woman getting the upper hand. Aranha laughed and stepped forward, leaning in close. "You still don't get it, I'm not here to do your bidding. I'm hungry and *you* are my dinner."

She opened her mouth then and let her black fangs extend to their full length. He started to struggle again, but she was quick to wrap a few more rounds of web around his upper body and legs. She stepped back and assessed, enjoying the fear in his eyes, knowing that he had seen it in his victims and hadn't cared, hadn't stopped. Sweat was running down his forehead and if his mouth hadn't been covered in web, she knew she'd hear more than just his muffled screaming.

"I would show you mercy, if I thought that you had ever shown any." She leaned in close, met his gaze straight on and reveled in the fear she saw there. "How many women did you destroy?"

He shook his head emphatically, his eyes pleading. He was realizing now that he was in trouble, that he was at her mercy, but she had no mercy for his kind. She bit his neck and his body convulsed in pain as her venom entered his bloodstream. It would slowly dissolve his insides, then she could come back and drink his fluids. It wasn't pretty, but it was nature, it's what she was. The poison worked quickly to stop his heart and his struggling, his suffering was nothing compared to what he had caused others, that was her only regret. She couldn't really make him feel what he'd done to his victims, but at least he was stopped.

Ten minutes later, he was completely wrapped in webbing, dead, and his insides were liquefying. He would be a nice little package for her to come back to in a few days when she got hungry.

She turned from him and was shocked to see Dag standing in the room watching her without expression. "What the hell are you doing?" she hissed, grabbing a knife from her side, ready to be attacked.

"I have questions." He spoke soft and calm, not reacting to her defensive stance.

"Yeah? Well I don't owe you any answers. He's dead by the way, he can't harm any more young women and the world is better off. You're welcome."

"Okay, where did you come from?"

"I don't owe you any answers," she repeated firmly, meeting his inquisitive gaze with a glare.

"You shouldn't exist, your species was hunted to extinction."

"So you're here to kill me, is that it?" She grabbed another knife, holding one in each hand, crouched and baring her fangs. She wouldn't go down without a fight. She didn't relish the idea of killing him, but she *would* protect herself. She had a duty to Jonah, if she just never returned he'd think she'd abandoned him and that would destroy him.

Dag took a deep breath and relaxed his shoulders. "I want answers, I don't want to kill you. I know not all webmakers are indiscriminate killers. It seems perhaps you know what you're doing. Who taught you?"

She ignored his statements, she didn't want to care what he knew or wanted to know. "How did you find me?"

"I know your scent now, you'll never be able to hide. It's subtle, but now that I know it, I can track you easily."

She thought about that, she wanted more than anything to just run, to hide and go to another city with Jonah. Would he really bother following her across the country, or world? There were plenty of places where psychopaths resided and needed culling. More of a danger, would be him telling others of her existence. Her mother had drilled the need to hide into her before she'd died. She might be able to hide from this one, but she couldn't hide from them all if they knew she was out there.

"What do you want to know?" She relaxed her stance but she didn't put the knives away, she didn't trust him. Maybe if she listened to him she could be sure he would keep her secret, or she might have to kill him.

He smiled. "Can we go somewhere else?"

Aranha looked back at her marinating meal. She had no desire to stay here. "What do you have in mind?" She couldn't exactly invite him back to her place, Jonah would probably freak, maybe try to protect her and get himself killed in the process.

"Come back to my place, its safe. I have no desire to harm you if you don't try to harm me."

"I thought I was supposed to lure you into *my* web," she laughed but she didn't really feel it, this situation was dangerous.

He held up his hands in a show of peace. "I promise, I am only interested in talking to you. I think—I think we may be able to help each other." He spoke slowly as if he were trying to figure it out for himself still.

She didn't like the idea of being in his space, but the public was no place for this conversation. She didn't trust him, but she *was* curious as to what he could possibly think she needed his help with, and how did *he* even exist? She had as many questions as he did, she was sure. She couldn't keep Jonah and herself safe if she didn't know what was out there; maybe he wasn't the only one and she needed to be aware of them as a danger too. She decided she had no better option. "I will follow you," she agreed.

He nodded and held the door open for her gallantly.

She didn't move. "I said I'll follow you."

"You should trust me," he said quietly.

His blue eyes stared straight into hers, it touched her soul and she had to steel herself against the threat of feelings she had no use for. "Why?" she hissed.

"I don't think you have anyone else," he said quietly, then

went out the door and up the stairs.

She bristled at the truth in his words. Other than Jonah, she didn't have anyone, but she didn't have to trust *him*, she had no reason to think he meant her anything other than harm. She tucked her knives away and locked the door behind them. Three brown spiders crept out of the dark and looked up at her. "Cover the door, make sure it looks unused and unwelcoming."

They moved quickly to do her bidding and she mounted the stairs with quick strides. "Where do you live?"

"Not in this shitty part of town, we'll have to drive."

"If it's so bad, then why do you have a business down here?"

"Same reason you hunt those who haunt this part of the city; privacy from other supernatural eyes, and deserving prey." He shrugged.

"You said you don't kill," she challenged, hoping to catch him in a lie. Something to grasp onto to tell her he wasn't what he was trying to present himself to be.

"Rarely, not in many years actually."

"How old are you?"

"I thought I was the one who had questions." He shot a smile over his shoulder.

"Are you like a million years old?" she shot back, angry at her own body's reaction to that smile.

"I'm five hundred and twenty-eight."

"Yikes, old man."

"Right... and you are?"

"Two hundred and sixteen."

"Just a young thing." He winked at her over his shoulder and she resisted the urge to stick her tongue out at him. Something about him made her feel light and playful; she didn't like it. She had to always be on guard, to always be watchful and wary, it was how she survived. She also knew there was a very good chance she would have to kill him to keep herself and

Jonah safe. She always had to keep that in mind, survival was the number one priority.

He led her behind the now dark and empty bar to his parked car. A sleek black thing with leather interior. "Nice," she admitted grudgingly as she slipped into the passenger seat.

"Thanks, I can't help splurging on a few things."

"The bar is pretty profitable?"

"Something like that," he mumbled and she was immediately on alert, her fingers twitched and she spread a web between her fingers.

Fuck you! He was shouting in his head while staring forward with a wry smile. He knew what she was doing.

She crushed the web and stared out the window as they passed rows of buildings. "You do realize that my venom could take you down, right?"

"Is that right? One of the only dangers to other immortals, it's what got so many webmakers killed, isn't it?"

"That's what I was told," she said stiffly.

"You might want to save your threats, I don't wish you harm and so I have no reason to fear you, isn't that what you claim? You only kill the dregs of society, and those who wish you harm?"

"Something like that. How do you pick *your* victims?"

"I don't kill."

"But you harm, that doesn't make it better if you are harming innocents. You can live through a hell of a lot, doesn't mean it's better than death," she said quietly, thinking of poor Jonah.

He looked at her then, his blue eyes flashing and his lips curled in a half smile that made her stomach flip and her thighs quiver. "Sweetie, what I do, it rarely feels like anything other than pleasure."

He turned back to look at the road and she was thankful he

couldn't see her face in the dark. Her cheeks flamed as images infiltrated her head that she wished she could blame on someone else. They were all hers, and she resented them, knew they couldn't come true, not without a risk she was no longer willing to take. She had someone who was relying on her, who would miss her if she just didn't come home. That kept her from courting too much danger.

They drove on in silence for a while, but she couldn't help wondering about him. "Why are you here?"

"In New York?"

"Yes, why here? There is a large population of vampires here, I didn't think daywalkers got along so well with them. Thought they killed you all off."

"Almost, we are the last clan. Most of us live up north in Connecticut."

"But not you?"

"No, I like a little more freedom."

She thought about that, would she choose to live with a group of webmakers given the choice, or would she feel oppressed? She doubted she wouldn't love it, the interaction with her own species, the comfort of being herself with others. "So there are more daywalkers?"

"Yes." He didn't offer explanation and she hated to seem curious, so she quit asking. She wanted to know how many, she wanted to know why the vampires and werewolves stopped trying to kill them. How the hell had the daywalkers survived but the webmakers hadn't?

The rest of the drive was silent and when they arrived at a large apartment building, she was surprised. It was fully functioning with a doorman and people coming and going, complete with underground parking and a security guard. Not what she expected to see at all. She'd imagined him holed up in a dilapidated mansion behind a black iron fence and unpruned bushes.

Something gothic and depressing, this was... almost glamourous. How the hell did he get to live like this?

"Mr. Larsen, welcome home." The guard at the garage waved and smiled as he pressed the button to lift the gate.

"Dag Larsen?"

"Yes, that is my name. You have yet to offer yours."

"Aranha Silva."

He laughed, "Portuguese for spider, not very original."

"My mother spent a lot of time in Portugal, I was born there."

"And came to America to pursue your dreams?" he prodded as he slid into a parking spot near the elevator.

"My mother brought me here when I was a baby."

"Just you and your mother? Easy to hide." He spoke as if he were connecting dots and she resented it a bit. She barely knew her history and him knowing more about her seemed invasive and unfair.

"Yes, for a time it was easy," she said quietly, not offering further explanation as memories of her mother assaulted her. They had settled into a small town for a few years before they were found out. She'd never stopped running after that.

"Aranha," Dag said softly and touched her arm, making her jump as she was dragged out of her sad memories.

"What do you want with me?" she hissed, feeling her fangs descend.

"I want to know why you exist and I want to know if you are more than a psychotic killing machine loose in my city." He took a deep breath. "I hope that you are, I think you are. Most webmakers weren't bloodthirsty killers."

"And if I am?" she challenged. She wanted it all out in the open. Did he intend to turn her over to the local vampires? She wasn't certain who was in charge in this city, she'd kept herself away from all other immortals so well that she couldn't tell if it was run by the vampires, or the werewolves; but by the sheer number she'd run into or smelled, she guessed vampire. She'd never considered it could be run by daywalkers of course, although that still seemed unlikely. Vampires were cunning and vicious, another reason she assumed they'd taken charge. Werewolves were... well they were good followers. She almost smiled thinking of her own little werewolf at home, she never would have thought she'd like having anyone around, especially a clingy werewolf.

Dag didn't respond, just got out of the car and walked around to open her door. She let him act the gentleman, it gave her a second to take a deep breath and calm her nerves. She followed him to the elevator and watched him punch in a code for the penthouse. He had money, that was for sure. She was a little jealous. She'd never been able to keep much money because she had to move so often, only stealing from those she killed to pay her way. She was ashamed to admit she'd also stolen from others in the past when necessary. Her choices were so limited. It was easy to filter a pin code from a mind at the ATM then follow them and slip the card out of a pocket or purse. Though she only resorted to that when she was truly desperate, which was more often since she'd brought Jonah home, he needed regular food she had to pay for.

The elevator stopped at the lobby and an elderly woman stepped on, smiling at Dag and giving Aranha a curious look before holding her purse a little tighter.

"Mrs. Willford, how are you this evening?" Dag said in the most pleasant voice she'd heard come out of him.

"Oh wonderful, just returning from the theater. My niece was in the show you know! She'll be a star one day," Mrs. Willford proclaimed.

"With you to mentor her, I have no doubt." Dag's tone was light and teasing and the woman's eyes lit up with pleasure.

"Oh, aren't you the sweetest?" she crooned, then got out on the fifth floor. "See you later, Dag dear."

"Have a good night, Mrs. Willford."

The elevator door slid shut and Aranha couldn't help commenting. "You don't look the type to live in a place like this."

"I don't just live here."

She eyed him skeptically, eyebrow raised and lips pursed. "So we are here because…"

"I own the building, and the top floor is my home." His chest puffed a little in pride.

"And yet you choose to run a dive bar in the worst part of town?" She was legitimately confused.

"Easy prey, remember," he winked and his eyes lit up. "Don't you know you shouldn't hunt where you live?" he said with another wink.

She hated to admit how attractive she found him when he did that shit, and the fact that he was doing it on purpose made it all the more annoying. "And out of the way of vampires," she added a little more aggressively than she intended.

He raised an eyebrow and gave her a half smile. "Exactly."

She didn't trust him, didn't understand him; and it terrified her that she was about to be alone with him in his personal space. The press of cold steel against her flesh was a comforting reminder that she wasn't unarmed. She wouldn't go down without a fight and if his intentions weren't to talk then he would seriously regret it.

CHAPTER FIVE

Dag knew his apartment was a bit cluttered, but it was comfortable. His treasures from around the world were everywhere. He'd amassed many in his long lifetime. Some of the furniture was as old as she was, some younger but still with an ornate and comfortable flair. Nothing could be called modern in here and he loved it.

"Nice place," she said with a nod of approval.

"Thanks, I like to collect things I guess. Hazard of immortality means I've collected a *lot* of stuff."

Aranha gave his joke a small chuckle as she walked around and continued to eye his things. He just watched her, something about having her appreciate his home gave him great pleasure. After a few minutes, she claimed a seat and looked at him expectantly.

He took a seat opposite her and leaned back, hoping he was giving off an air of relaxation. He needed her trust—more importantly, he *wanted* it. "So let's start with how do you even still exist? Your species was supposed to have been eradicated nearly three hundred years ago."

"It nearly was. As far as I know my mother and I were the last when I was born. She died when I was still young."

"How did she die?"

"Vampires."

Her answer didn't surprise him at all, vampires feared webmakers and daywalkers. "You haven't seen another of your kind, not ever?"

"No, and my mother was no murderer either. She's the one who taught me how to find the ones who are truly evil, who deserve to be taken off the planet. I've never killed for any reason other than to save another, not even if I was starving."

"How often do you eat?"

She glared and bristled at what she must have assumed was a trick to get her to confess to being a relentless killer. "How often do *you* eat, daywalker? And on the subject of existence, why aren't you all eradicated. I thought the vampires took you all out too."

He laughed then and folded his hands behind his head. She was not going to be an easy one to crack. "You can trust me, how can I make you believe that? I am trusting you and I deserve the same in kind."

"Why are you trusting me?" she demanded warily.

He smiled and leaned forward. He met her eyes and held them. "Because I need your help."

She looked uncomfortable but she didn't look away, her words were a whisper. "Why would I help you with anything?"

"Because you care about others in a general sense if what you say is true, and you would not leave another to suffer unnecessarily." He knew it was a bit of a leap, to assume this about her, but he was certain fate had brought her into his bar tonight, it wasn't just chance.

"Who is suffering that you can't save by yourself, big bad daywalker?" she lifted an eyebrow in a teasing manner.

She had a hard exoskeleton, but he was willing to bet her center was soft and warm. He couldn't stop his eyes from running down the length of her body and back up appreciatively.

"I don't know for certain. I only caught sight of her by accident once. From what I can tell though, she's a human and she is quite young, maybe eighteen and being held at the vampire compound north of the city. I was there for my monthly visit, paying protection money to the horde that rules this city." He expressed his distaste for the fact clearly in his voice. He didn't want her to think he was a willing ally of the vampires. "I like to fly under the radar, but I'm not invisible, so I play their game. I pay them and they let me do my thing without intrusion."

"So what do you care about their in-house meal?" she scoffed.

"I can't explain it, but there was something... something more about her. I don't think she is there of her own accord, of course, but it wasn't just sadness I sensed in her. She doesn't deserve whatever they're doing to her." Dag let his frustration be clear in his voice, he wanted her to know how seriously he was taking the situation. "I don't know what's going on, but I don't like it. The vampires have been moving a lot lately, haven't you noticed? A lot more of them have been coming into the city and they move in larger groups than before. They are getting ready for something, and I think it has something to do with the girl."

Aranha nodded. "I've noticed, I was thinking it was probably time to move on. Why should I care what the vampires are up to?"

"They are dangerous, and your venom is a very effective weapon against them."

"So I've heard. I have never tested the theory though. What do you even think we will do? Waltz in and fight a war? Two against two hundred? Your venom should be just as effective as mine by the way; you don't really need me to risk my life as well. I *am* an endangered species," she said the last with a laugh.

He couldn't help smiling. "I was thinking more along the lines of sneaking in for information, nothing too risky. How small can you get?"

Her eyes narrowed. "You want me to crawl in there in spider form! Are you nuts? They will sense me and squish me."

"Not during the day. You could sneak in while they sleep. You could leave some strategic webs, then collect them the next day. We could learn a lot in one night I bet. If I have proof of something, I could rally support. We wouldn't be going against them alone. We could save the girl from whatever fate they plan for her."

"They probably just want to turn her into a vampire," Aranha scoffed.

"If that were it, they would have done it by now. And before you ask, no, they aren't just feeding on her. I didn't see any marks on her neck and she didn't look like she was being drained. Humans that are used as livestock don't look good, they look sick and vacant in the eyes. She was all there, her eyes met mine briefly and she was—she was terrified and determined. I can't explain it, I just know it's something more and I need to help her."

Aranha sighed. "And what would become of me, after you out me to whatever army you amass in your efforts to save this human?"

"I would offer you my shield, Aranha." It was a great honor he was offering her and he expected her to be impressed. "If you are as honorable as you say you are, then I will die to protect you. I have no desire to let your species fall into extinction."

She burst out laughing; he did *not* expect that. "Sure, okay, I tell you what. I have a personal vendetta against vampires and I don't appreciate innocents being harmed. So I will go in during the day and lay some webs, but beyond that, I promise nothing. If it's too dangerous, I won't even go in and collect them, got it? I don't need your *shield* and I don't want to be saved. I just want to live my life."

His hands were gripping the arms of the chair so hard he knew he was probably denting the old wood. How dare she laugh at him for offering her the greatest honor he could, did she not understand? Of course not, he reasoned, she had no idea. She was raised by a single webmaker on the run, afraid of her own shadow and all the immortals that moved through it. This woman had no idea what the world of other immortals entailed, or what her place in it was. He had to tread very carefully or she would spook and she would run. No matter what he'd claimed, there was no way he'd find her if she really took off. He couldn't track her if she decided to take a plane to another continent, she'd be quite possibly lost to him forever and that thought was more frightening than he wanted to admit. "Fine, I won't mention you when I bring my evidence forward, unless it is absolutely necessary."

She looked like she was giving it some real thought. He could tell she wasn't fully convinced, and he wasn't sure what he would do if she said no. There was no way he could just let her walk out of his life now.

"When do we go?" she finally said, and he had to hold himself back from whooping with joy at his luck.

"I don't want to risk being out tonight, we will head out in the morning, sunrise. It's an hour from the city so they'll be deep asleep by the time we get there."

"I will meet you at sunrise." She stood to leave, eyeing him with distrust.

He wished he could force her to stay, to guarantee she wouldn't run before morning. "You'll want to feed before we go, just in case. I wouldn't want you to be caught with your strength down."

"You as well, I assume. Perhaps Mrs. Willford would be a willing sacrifice?" she teased as she passed him. "I'll be out front at sunrise."

After he closed the door behind her, he did a thorough search of her path to make sure she hadn't left any sneaky webs behind. He didn't want her in his head, not until he figured out what he was going to do about her.

When he was satisfied that she hadn't, he sunk onto the chair she'd vacated and let her scent surround him. He knew what he should do, what was expected of him. He should be calling Sten, alerting him to this new development. The presence of a webmaker was report worthy, but he just couldn't bring himself to do that. She was a miracle and Sten was a loose cannon.

No, he had to make sure she had provided invaluable information before he alerted Sten. There had to be a reason for Sten to think twice about how to proceed with her. She was more than just the last webmaker, she was a warrior and should be treated as such. It didn't matter if this particular warrior made his blood run hot and his mind fill with lascivious thoughts. All the more reason to not tell Sten or anyone else about her.

When his phone rang an hour later, he jumped and stared at it with a frown. This couldn't be good. He turned it over and saw Harold's face and groaned.

"What?" he answered, not caring to play nice.

"Why the fuck is your bar closed?"

"I didn't feel like being there tonight."

"Yeah well, I do, so come open up."

"Find your meal somewhere else."

"Sten has a message for you."

Dag held back a groan, he'd been avoiding Sten for the last few weeks. "What is it?"

"He wants you to present yourself to him tomorrow."

"I'm busy."

Harold just laughed. No one denied Sten. He was in charge of the daywalkers. "I'll tell him to expect you in the afternoon. That should give you plenty of time to get to Connecticut."

Harold hung up before Dag could say anything else. He had no choice and they both knew it. He'd been denying Sten for too long.

Could he protect Aranha from Sten?

Dag left his condo in a rage. His life was his own, he'd worked hard for it, but no matter what, Sten could swoop in and start calling the shots.

Control, Dag sought it the only way he knew how; stalking the vulnerable on the street. He followed a young male prostitute into a dark alley, Dag would leave the poor soul some money and a good memory as payment for the blood he took. It was as fair as he could get, and it was survival.

Aranha hurried home, she had to take a bus but that didn't really bother her. She had a lot on her mind and closing her eyes while it drove, gave her time to consider everything that had happened. It was overwhelming. Daywalkers existed, and at least this one, didn't want to kill her on sight—that didn't make him safe though, she reminded herself. His venom could kill and if he told anyone else about her, she could end up dead.

She didn't have an answer to that line of thought so she switched to what she was going to tell Jonah about being out of the house tomorrow during the day. If she ever left during the day, she always took him with her. She'd learned early on that unless she was hunting, she couldn't get him to stay back without him going into massive emo pout mode. It was like a deep dark spiral into the hell that was his existence without her in it and it usually took them back a few steps from him ever being independent enough to leave her.

When she got to the apartment, she knocked their secret knock; three sharp raps, then two slow. That way he wouldn't freak out when she came in. They'd had a few instances when he was first there; she'd come in suddenly and he'd gone full werewolf from the fright. Now, although he was much calmer and more in control than before, she still did the knock just in case. One accidental bite from him and she would be in trouble.

"Aranha," he shouted and jumped off the couch to greet her. There was always a bit of surprise in his eyes when she walked in, no matter how many times she assured him that she wasn't going to leave him. His entire self-worth was wrapped up in her and she knew that wasn't healthy, she just didn't know how to fix it. She assumed it was a wolf thing, she'd become his alpha and his mother; in his mind, he was nothing she didn't tell him to be.

"Did you have a good evening?" she asked, giving him a quick peck on the cheek. "Did you go out and find a wild woman to steal your heart, or at least some of your time?"

"Yeah, right," he blushed. "I was just about to dye my hair, you should help me!"

"Only if you let me cut it too," she said with a smile, she'd been trying to get him to let her trim it for six months, but he'd refused. She playfully pulled on a strand.

"What's that smell?" he sniffed her with a frown, then walked around her, sniffing some more. "What did you get into? That's not human I smell," he accused.

She bristled at his accusatory tone. "Not that it's any of your business, but I met a daywalker tonight."

His face fell, shame filled his eyes and he backed away, hanging his head. "Sorry, Ma'am," he whispered.

She sighed heavily, "Jonah, you're not in trouble for being curious. I was only teasing," she lied. She wasn't used to explaining herself to anyone and she didn't want Jonah to get any alpha attitude with her, that would never work for their relationship.

"Oh... do you want to cut my hair?" he asked to make amends for the perceived offense.

Aranha shook her head and touched his chin, lifting his eyes to hers. "I think it looks great, let's add some blue and I'll tell you all about my night. I met an extinct species and I took down a murderer."

He smiled brightly and hurried to the bathroom. She followed, wondering how long until the mother werewolf was supposed to kick the baby out of the den. Of course if he wasn't traumatized he might not have stuck around more than a couple of days, but he had, and her solitary lifestyle wasn't exactly conducive to him branching out either. She really did wish he would go out and try to get laid some night, it would do him good.

She told him about her night as she dyed his hair and he grew more and more concerned. "I will go with you," he said firmly.

"I don't think that would be a good idea, I don't want to put you in danger. He might see you as a threat, daywalkers don't get along with werewolves."

"Neither do webmakers, according to you," he pointed out. "But here we are." He smiled up at her as she rinsed his hair in the tub, blue dye swirling down the drain.

She tried to sound as serious as the situation required. "I don't know what we might run into tomorrow. We are heading to a vampire compound with werewolf guards, that's dangerous if they smell you. A solitary werewolf could be seen as a major threat to the pack."

"Then you need me to back you up. You don't even know this guy, he could be a complete psycho." He ignored her comment about him being in danger.

She wanted to argue, but he had a point. He could definitely be of assistance if Dag decided to change plans and kidnap or kill her, and maybe a little adventure would be just the thing to help get Jonah out of this paralyzing state of need, too.

"Okay, but you have to be *very* careful. I don't know if I trust this guy or not and it *will* be dangerous where we're going."

"I will always protect you," Jonah vowed solemnly, again completely missing her point.

"I know you will, darling." She smiled down at him because she didn't know what else to say, "and your hair looks fucking awesome."

His smile was bright and she melted a bit, this little werewolf had really stolen her heart. She smiled back and handed him a towel.

"Whoa! I look fierce!" He exclaimed to his reflection.

"Very fierce," and not at all inconspicuous she added to herself.

"Do you think he will like me?" he asked suddenly.

"Doesn't matter," she said quickly before realizing his fear came from his past experiences with males and not a wish for friendship.

His head hung slightly and he picked at the black polish on his nails. "Yeah, doesn't matter."

"What I mean is, I love you and he doesn't have to like you, but he does have to be nice, to both of us, because we are helping him. He won't hurt you, because if he does, I'll kill him," she said firmly and she knew it was true. No one got to hurt her werewolf boy.

"I love you too, Aranha," he said quietly, embarrassed.

He always acted shy when she told him she loved him, she didn't do it often, but she meant it with her whole being when she said it. She pulled him in for a hug. "Let's watch a movie."

They settled on the couch and watched the original Teen Wolf; it was his favorite.

CHAPTER SIX

Aranha and Jonah stood in the shadows across from Dag's building as the sun came up. She more than half hoped he just didn't show. She kept telling herself they should have made a run for it; he couldn't track her forever, but she just couldn't. Her mother had uprooted and taken them across the country for a *new adventure,* so many times. She didn't want to do that to Jonah if she could help it. When she was thirteen she stopped feeling like it was an adventure and started to hate it. That's when her mother decided to risk staying somewhere, and they'd had a few very good years.

Then a werewolf had followed her home one day. He'd been working in the village, doing some repairs, and Aranha had trusted him, had let him see her spin a web. She didn't understand his reaction, the thoughts she'd caught from him had confused and terrified her. She so desperately didn't want to move again though; she was sixteen and she was in love with a human boy in town. That one selfish decision had changed everything.

She looked at Jonah, he was dressed head to toe in black, even a black beanie covered most of his newly blue hair. Dragging him unnecessarily around the world to stay hidden was not going to help his depression or anxiety. So here they were, she wasn't making selfish decisions, she was doing what was best for him.

His eyes were cautious and bright, scanning for danger in the glow of the morning sun. There was an excitement in him, he needed adventure beyond a trip to the grocery store. He needed friends, and a girlfriend, she just had no idea how to go about making those things happen. She wondered briefly if she should hire him a prostitute, just to get him a little action. If it wasn't too dangerous, she'd enroll him in college, maybe someday.

Dag pulled up in front of her and rolled down the passenger window, he looked from her to Jonah curiously. "Aranha, I'm glad to see you showed up."

Jonah immediately stepped close to Aranha, slightly behind and growled at Dag. Dag looked surprised but not scared. "Dag, this is Jonah, he's... he's my son, adopted."

The shocked look on Dag's face was intense but he quickly covered it with an easy smile. "Hey Jonah, as long as you're housebroken, you're welcome to join."

Jonah growled, Aranha laughed. "He's harmless, just protective."

Dag's eyes looked purposefully at the way Jonah was cowered slightly behind Aranha and tilted his head slightly. "I can see that," he said with forced seriousness.

She bent down to the window and peered inside. He was dressed casually in jeans and a t-shirt, his blond hair was half up in a sort of messy bun and half loose around his shoulders. "It's a long story, but he isn't dangerous as long as you aren't." She winked at him.

"I am very dangerous." He winked back. "You getting in?"

He gave her a full smile and she was struck by the way it lit up his blue eyes.

"I guess we don't really have a choice, do we?"

"Not kidnapping you," he laughed.

"Not yet," she grumbled as she opened the door. Jonah crawled into the small backseat and she got in the front. She dropped a bag on the floor that contained more than her usual amount of weaponry. She wasn't sure what they would face, but she was sure as hell not going to be caught without something to protect herself and Jonah with. She had the usual blades strapped to her body under her shorts and tank top and Jonah had some blades strapped on as well. She had taught him how to use them and he was pretty skilled, she would trust him to protect himself, and her if it came to it.

Dag eyed the bag curiously, but didn't say anything. "What kind of music do you like?" he asked over his shoulder.

"Anything is fine," Jonah said quietly. He was scooted all the way over to the side behind Aranha, leaning forward with one hand on her shoulder. She knew the touch was comforting for him. She reached up and patted his hand.

"Jonah likes alt rock."

Dag laughed and found a radio station.

She smiled out the window. Dag's kindness toward Jonah was unexpected.

They drove north, out of the city, at a fast pace. There wasn't much conversation to distract her, but she did everything she could to keep her thoughts on the mission at hand.

"So, what's the plan?" She broke the silence as they pulled off the main road and parked next to an eight-foot iron fence. Trees planted on the inside of the fence blocked all view of whatever was beyond it, but she imagined it was something resembling Dracula's castle.

"The compound is pretty large, walled in, obviously, with a

huge yard between the fence and the house. Werewolves stand guard during the day."

"And you expect me to crawl my ass across a huge lawn, around the werewolves, lay some webs inside, crawl back out—all before the sun goes down—undetected by the werewolves? Are you insane?" she scoffed.

Jonah whined in the back and gripped her shoulder harder. "It's too dangerous," he whispered.

"I was thinking maybe you could hitch a ride on a delivery truck actually. It comes through every morning, bringing supplies. It'll stop at the gate for inspection, then it'll drive on to the kitchen. They'll unload it for thirty minutes or so, then it'll leave. You need to be back on it when it leaves, you'll never be able to cross the yard as a spider in time."

"It's too risky," Jonah whispered. "You shouldn't go."

Aranha knew her face was showing all the disbelief she was feeling, and she didn't care. She agreed with Jonah on this one. "This is a well thought out plan, what else are you hiding? I had assumed we were winging it." She didn't trust him.

"I thought about using the delivery truck to sneak myself in, yes, that plan was a thought before I met you. I've been watching the place for about a month now, getting the flow of things and noticing the changes."

She gave him a slow smile. "You would have been ripped to pieces."

"Exactly why I never went through with it," he hissed. Jonah whined at Dag's aggressive tone and pressed himself closer to the back of Aranha's seat. Dag rolled his eyes at the boy but when he spoke again his voice was softer. "Since you tried so hard to convince me you're not a merciless killer, I figured you were perfectly suited to the plan."

"Convenient. You will be waiting here patiently, I assume?"

"We will."

Aranha patted Jonah's hand and looked back at him. "Don't worry, Jonah." She turned back to Dag. "If you leave me here, I will hunt you down and I will pull your fangs out with a pair of rusty pliers."

"Fair enough, now you better get going, the truck is due anytime in the next twenty minutes or so."

"And how exactly do you expect me to get from the car to the gate where I am supposed to wait for and then hop aboard the truck?" she asked, a little exasperated.

He paused only a moment before answering. "Shift, I'll drive by slowly and you jump out the window."

"Are you fucking nuts! You want me to jump out of a moving vehicle?"

"Throw a web, don't spiders use webs to fly?"

She sighed heavily, his knowledge of spider activity was annoying and disconcerting. "Something like that."

"So it'll work?" he pressed.

"No way," Jonah said firmly.

"Theoretically. I can't control where I go though, if the wind takes me in another direction I'll miss the opportunity."

"Worth a shot I'd say, because the other option is I put you on the back of a paper airplane and toss that bitch over the wall."

Jonah growled at that statement and Dag gave him a stern look that shut him up immediately.

Aranha wanted to laugh, but the look on Dag's face was disturbingly serious. "We'll call that Plan C."

"What's Plan B?" he asked with a grin.

"I tell you to go fuck yourself, then Jonah and I find a new state to live in," she said sweetly as she started to undress.

"I like Plan B," Jonah whined in the back.

Dag looked back at him curiously then at Aranha. "How the hell did you get a werewolf to imprint on you so thoroughly?"

"Long story, and you don't need to know," she said with a smile. "But men make him nervous, so I expect you to be nice."

Dag huffed but let it drop.

Aranha could shift while dressed, but then she had to crawl out of her clothes, that could be a real pain, she avoided it when she wasn't in a real big hurry. Dag didn't look away as she started to strip, but it didn't really bother her until she was down to her underwear and bra. Jonah was staring out the side window, he always gave her ample privacy, even though she'd never asked for it. Aranha turned away and unhooked the bra, letting it drop on the floor of the car, then she shifted quickly. She didn't miss his gasp as she shrunk and twisted into the shape of a spider. She crawled out of her thong with eight long legs around a black body with silver streaks down her abdomen. She liked to spend time in this form, it was freeing to not pretend to be anything other than what she was. No one noticed a spider in a dark corner just existing.

She started to climb up to the open window. She perched on the windowsill and turned to look at him. His face was curious and it took everything she had not to spin out a little web and capture whatever it was he was thinking.

"She's pretty as a spider, isn't she?" Jonah said quietly. His face was resting on the seat now, getting as close as he could to her. His eyes were locked onto her and full of sadness.

"She's an impressive arachnid," Dag said and started the car. They waited like that until the delivery truck passed. "I hope you're ready, better hold on." He pulled onto the road behind the truck and followed at a short distance. Dag slowed as the delivery truck made it's turn, she shot out a line of web and leapt out the window. She could hear Jonah whine as she went.

The wind caught her and she found herself clinging to the back of the van after a short moment in the air. She hurried to a shady spot on the bumper and spun a bit of web to help hold her in place when the truck started to move again. She could hear the murmur of voices as the driver exchanged pleasantries with the guard, but she couldn't tell what they were saying. It probably wasn't *Hey, can you eat the spider lady on the back of my truck please*. So she didn't worry about trying to get closer to hear.

As the truck moved forward, she caught sight of the werewolf at the gate. He was a very large man dressed in all black with a gun strapped to his belt. Bald head, sunglasses, and a face that looked like he'd been in a brawl or two recently. She was guessing the other guy was dead. He sniffed the air as the truck passed and looked at it sharply, he even lifted his glasses and squinted in the direction of the truck.

Shit! was all she could think of, he smelled her and he was going to alert someone at the house. She was going to be discovered and squished under a boot, or forced to fight naked.

But the werewolf put his glasses back on and turned away, closing the gate. She sighed in relief at her luck, though she knew it might not hold out. Werewolves had a very sensitive sense of smell and if the house was full of them, she could still be in trouble.

She figured her best bet would be getting into the duct system and letting her scent trail through the whole house so that they wouldn't be able to pinpoint her location, of course that would take her knowing something about this place she was headed and having time to spare. She was unfortunately blind going in and had very little time to do the job she needed to do.

She lucked out again, the truck spun around and backed up to a door. She was able to scramble off and hide near the building door quickly. She watched as the driver walked around and opened up the back of the truck. He was a short man, kind of mousy in the face and walked with a slight limp. He was definitely human and he didn't look excited about being here. He opened the back of the truck and she hissed. She wasn't expecting to see three gagged and bound humans sitting on top of crates in the back of the truck, though she shouldn't have been surprised, what other kinds of things would vampires need delivered on a regular basis? They looked like they were asleep sitting up, she would bet they were drugged. They also looked like they'd been picked up on the street corner last night; all wearing high heels and party dresses that looked haggard and worn. No doubt they were prostitutes that no one would miss.

She wished she could help them, and promised them silently that she would return to free them as soon as she could, if it wasn't too late. She was useless to them now, alone and naked, not a good way to fight she reminded herself. She scurried into a kitchen when the door opened and two werewolves walked out. Both huge, both wearing all black. One blond, the other had red hair, both had looks that showed zero tolerance for bullshit. She had no interest in drawing their attention and hated that she had to leave those humans to their mercy.

"Ben! Good to see you back, man. How was your little vacation?" the blond wolf said, slapping the driver on the back.

"Yeah, I hear you were taking it easy in the ICU for a week," the redhead said with a laugh.

Aranha could only mutter in her mind, *asshole wolves*. Before she'd met Jonah, she'd thought they were all the same; violent, and quick to overreact. Now she knew it wasn't just instinctual, it was learned behavior and most learned to be this. They were a danger to everyone around them, which is why vampires liked them so much, they were also loyal. She was angered by the possibility that there was a poor, human girl in the house, innocent and being forced to deal with these werewolves and vampires. Aranha's resolve to help notched up. She didn't have much time, it didn't seem like there was much in the truck to unload and Ben didn't seem likely to hang out and chat after.

Figuring she had more like twenty than thirty minutes, she created a web under the kitchen counter. She kept on alert, listening to everything going on around her. There were voices deeper in the house; she couldn't make out what they were saying, but that didn't matter, it told her there were more than the three werewolves working during the day. She tried to distinguish the voices and get some kind of count; she was sure it would be useful to know later on. Her best guess was at least two others in the house. Plus the three she'd seen made at least five werewolves and who knew how many vampires in the house. That was a lot in a fight.

Blondie hauled a motionless prostitute through the kitchen, followed by the redhead with a crate he dropped and pushed under the counter with his foot, nearly taking out her perfectly placed web. When he walked back outside, she jumped down and scrambled out of the kitchen through a doorway she'd watched Blondie go through with the prostitute.

She was in a hallway lined with doors and a soft, blood red carpet. The walls were cream wallpaper with stripes of gold. It had a very Victorian feel, befitting vampires. It bothered her that these monsters lived in such luxury and she'd had an entire long life of living in shabby small homes, trying to survive and squeak by unnoticed, it wasn't fair. She tried very hard to *not* be a monster, what was it benefitting her? If she pushed Jonah out, would he join up with a pack of werewolves and live like this too? Serve vampires in luxurious surroundings instead of watching a small television in a crumbling apartment? It pissed her off, where was the balance of good intentions and rewards?

Aranha left a web under a small side table as she grumbled to herself. Blondie came back down the hall and out to the kitchen, to grab another prisoner, she assumed. From her vantage she could see there were four doors in the hall and it looked like it ended at a front entryway with stairs going up and most likely a large living area to the right and left. She wanted to go that far but it seemed risky. Blondie was already back with the second prostitute, Aranha's time was running out very fast.

She slipped into the nearest room, it had a large enough crack at the bottom of the door to allow her to wiggle under. She emerged into a small office with an antique desk and a glass cabinet that housed a collection of skulls that looked far from ancient.

She laid a web under a chair near the door, then raced back out. She would have loved to investigate deeper, but the risk of not getting back off the property was too great, so she scurried toward the truck. She had no desire to remain in this house until tomorrow when the delivery truck returned, everything about the place screamed vampire and completely creeped her out. Blondie was back for the third girl and the redhead had finished unloading the crates, but he was keeping Ben in conversation about someone they knew by the name of Jane.

Don't stop talking. Aranha pleaded mentally as she raced along edges and darted through open spaces as quick and silent as she could. The riskiest part was going to be getting up on the truck from the ground. She'd have to climb a tire and if he started to drive; she shuddered, she really didn't want to end up squashed over this.

"Jane says you won't let her quit her job, what's up with that?" Redhead was saying to Ben.

"What am I supposed to do, Billy?"

The redhead's name is Billy! What a dumb name for a werewolf. Aranha scoffed to herself as she made the climb to safety.

"I have to pay for medical bills now, and Sarah's wedding is coming up. Jane can't quit the bar, not this year," Ben whined.

"My sister shouldn't be forced to serve assholes all night,

Ben. I don't like it!"

"Then maybe you should tell the boss to pay me more. I get the girls, I deliver the girls, and the other supplies, I risk everything and what do I get?"

"Yeah, I'll tell him," Billy laughed. "You better get going, we need four more for tomorrow."

"Four! I can't get four. Do you have any idea how hard three was? The street walkers are starting to get suspicious. They see my van coming and they're hiding if they have any sense left in 'em."

"Then get creative, the boss is planning a party and they need it catered."

Ben huffed, but didn't argue. He just shut the back of the truck and walked back to the cab. Aranha was tucked in semi safety by the time the truck rumbled to start and made its way back down the driveway. The vampires were planning a party, that must be why so many were in town, but what did they have to celebrate and what did it have to do with the human girl prisoner?

The truck barely stopped at the gate before barreling out to the main road, no parting conversation with the guard at the gate. Aranha had to make a quick decision to jump, letting out a length of web to catch the wind, she was whipped into the air and found herself landing about six feet up a tree. At least she was out of sight of the gate, and she wasn't attached to someone's windshield. Now she had to decide; take the long slow crawl down, or risk a naked tree descent just a foot off the main road.

When she saw Dag drive by, glaring out into the trees, she decided on naked. Jonah wasn't visible in the back seat and panic welled up inside of her. She shifted back to human and scrambled out of the tree as fast as she could, managing to cut a decent size gash in her upper thigh.

CHAPTER SEVEN

Dag felt his mouth go dry, his heart stop beating, and his pants tighten as he saw her standing on the side of the road. About two feet off the pavement, next to a tree. Naked. Head to toe naked, with her silvery hair blowing in the slight breeze. She was a dream and now he knew that tattoo of hers did go all the way down. He'd seen it in the car seconds before she'd shifted and nearly lost his breath. It was a huge spider web tattoo covering her entire back, it was gorgeous and dammit, so was she. A fierce possessiveness filled him as he looked at her, in plain sight of anyone passing. He wanted to kill anyone who might look at her. "Fuck," he grumbled. He didn't want to want her, but his body fiercely disagreed with that logic.

His eyes swept the full length of her as he stopped on the side of the road, assessing her wellbeing. She was bleeding. The sweet smell of her blood wafted into the car and his fangs descended in response to all the stimulation. "Are you alright?" he hissed as she jumped in the car.

"Where's Jonah? Get out of here, the guard could smell me and now I'm bleeding, too."

"Yeah, I caught that." He knew his words were coming out

harsh but he couldn't help it, it was taking every ounce of control he had not to pull over and attack her.

"A gentleman would put his fangs away in the company of a lady," she hissed back as she started to yank on her clothes.

"Who said I was a gentleman?" He slammed the car in gear and spun out, off down the road.

"Where's Jonah?" she hissed again.

"Relax, I wouldn't harm him. He is insanely attached to you though, I don't think it's healthy." Jonah had whined the whole time Aranha had been out of the car. It was like having a puppy in the backseat! It nearly drove Dag to screaming. He'd never witnessed a werewolf attachment like that, it was usually much more subtle and toward another werewolf. He didn't know their story, but he was willing to bet it was interesting.

"Rough childhood. Where is he?" she hissed again, not letting the attitude go, not trusting him, and it made him want to scream at her and shake her.

"There are napkins in the glovebox," he hissed instead. "Can you at least *try* to stop the bleeding."

"Sure, when you tell me where Jonah is," she snapped.

He had nothing left to hold him back, her attitude was the last straw. He hit the brakes and the car spun off the road, making a full circle and pointing north again. He moved faster than she could react. One arm went across her chest, just below her breasts, pinning her back against the seat and her arms down, his other hand gripped her knee below her bleeding thigh. His head dipped and his tongue slid across the weeping wound. His fangs dripped healing venom and ached to slide into her flesh. He resisted the urge but didn't miss a drop of blood that escaped the now quickly closing gap. His body was on fire as the taste of her rushed through him. It was better than anything he'd ever experienced and pulled on something so deep; he didn't want to investigate it. As he pulled back, he let his tongue graze the wound one last time and was rewarded with the feel of her body shuddering.

"Don't fuck with me, Aranha," he hissed, then slammed the car back in gear.

She spoke so quietly, he wasn't sure he was hearing her at first. "The next time you decide to handle me like that, I will stick a blade in you before I fill you full of venom that will melt your insides while you scream for mercy."

His lip twitched into a smile and she growled. He was filled with satisfaction at the thought that she had been so disturbed by her answering reaction to his touch, that she had missed the fact that he'd dripped venom into her open wound to help her heal.

"Jonah was running along the other side of the road looking for you, I figured it was best to cover more ground in case you hadn't jumped right away," he explained.

It didn't take long to find him, the only goth kid loping along the side of the highway. His eyes were huge and frightened and when he hurried to the passenger door he was panting. He leaped through the open window into Aranha's lap, nuzzling her neck. "Why do I smell blood?"

Dag couldn't understand their relationship, knew it wasn't sexual, but he was jealous of it anyway. He hadn't been that close to anyone in a long time, maybe not ever. He tried to remember when he was young, when he'd had his mother and father close, did it feel like what they seemed to have? His father had been tough, a warrior and he didn't show much affection. His mother had been sweet and caring, but distracted, those were dangerous times.

"Cut my leg on a tree," she said softly, patting his hair. "Get in back so we can go home."

Jonah crawled in back unwillingly. "Did it go well?"

"Yes, was Dag nice while I was gone?"

"Yes," he said almost grudgingly.

Dag rolled his eyes at her, then started driving again. North.

"You're going the wrong way."

"I have another meeting, you two will just have to tag along. I don't have time to take you back to the city."

"I don't take kindly to being kidnapped," she said carefully, and Jonah growled. "Where are we going?" she demanded.

"I have to see Sten, but don't worry, I didn't plan on introducing you two." He really didn't, and he hated that he had to take her anywhere near the daywalker compound, but if he didn't go it would only cause Sten and the others to seek him out. More daywalkers in the city to possibly run across Aranha was not a better option.

Aranha glared at Dag. "Who's Sten?"

"Daywalker, leader of what's left of us, self-proclaimed king."

"Sten will try to kill me," she hissed. This was *not* part of the plan and it was a *very* bad idea. She didn't want to overreact, but she was very close to grabbing Jonah and jumping out of a moving vehicle.

Dag laughed, "Probably not."

She wanted to lash out at him, but didn't want to risk him crashing the car. "And yet you're bringing me there anyway?"

Jonah growled in the backseat.

"I have no choice," he said with a frustrated sigh.

"Ah, you've been *summoned*. You answer to a vampire and a daywalker. You aren't your own man, Dag. How disappointing," she sneered, knowing it would piss him off.

His face hardened and his knuckles went white on the steering wheel. She couldn't help a little smile, knowing she'd hit it on the head, he was under someone's control and he didn't like it one bit. Well, neither did she, but here they were.

"Why must you see him today?" she prodded.

"My business with Sten is none of yours," he hissed.

She let that sit for a while, thinking about all that had occurred in the last twelve hours. She could respect his *I work alone* mentality more if he wasn't basically kidnapping her after coercing her into helping him. She decided to trust him anyway.

"They are bringing in prostitutes to the compound. Three were in the van tonight and I heard them ask for four more for a party tomorrow night. What do you think that means?"

"I think it means they're planning a party," he said sharply.

She shot him a dark glare but his eyes were straight ahead and it was wasted. "Gee, why didn't I think of that."

"Isn't that why you laid the webs? To help me figure out what's going on in there, what they're planning with the girl?" he sounded exasperated.

"If I'm bothering you, you're welcome to pull over, we'll find our own way back to the city," she said with a bright smile.

He turned to her then, his face stone. "I don't plan on letting you out of my sight again until those webs are retrieved and interpreted."

"And here I thought you *weren't* kidnapping me. And how do you plan to keep me in line? You do know that if I chose to, I could easily kill you."

"I'm no vampire," he said with a harsh laugh. "I'm a daywalker, your venom won't kill me and I dare you to try." He let his fangs protrude as he gave her a wide smile.

She sat back, unsure if he was telling the truth. Were daywalkers immune to her venom? If that were true, she could be in some serious trouble walking into a compound of them.

"Mine could," Jonah said quietly but they both ignored him.

"It's because I was never human," he explained. "Webmaker

venom kills all mortal beings, vampires were once mortal. Webmakers and daywalkers though, we were never mortal, we are the original species and we can't kill each other that way. You aren't susceptible to my venom either, which is why I used it to help heal up your leg. How is it that you don't know this?"

She glanced down at her healed wound and frowned then stared out the passenger window, how had she missed that? Her body had been vibrating with unwelcome delight, that's how. There were a lot of things her mother didn't have a chance to teach her, this was one of those things she'd assumed. Incorrectly, apparently. She refused to ask him to explain, but he continued anyway, sensing her confusion.

"Legend says there were two in the garden at the beginning of time, a man who gained his power from the sun, a daywalker, and a woman who wove webs of magic, a webmaker. Which is why all daywalkers are male and all webmakers are female. Together they created children, daywalkers and webmakers. There were humans of course, for food. Eventually the humans split off, fearing their place in the garden and on the food chain. They ate from the forbidden tree, thinking it was key to gaining magic and elevating themselves from prey to predator. When they were thrown out of the garden and into the world that became man's, they forgot all about the possibility of magic, it was erased from their memories. They now believe that they top the food chain," he laughed darkly.

"When did the daywalkers and webmakers get kicked out?" Aranha asked, unable to stop her curiosity.

"The legend says that they learned prejudice when the others left. The daywalkers blamed the webmakers and the webmakers blamed the daywalkers. Their hatred of each other grew and they stopped breeding which angered the gods who created us to love each other. They threw us out as punishment. We landed in the world of men but we were so few and they were so many that we had to hide and for the first time, we had an enemy capable of killing us."

"So that's where the werewolves and vampires come in?" She patted Jonah's hand which was on her shoulder, he was listening intently to all of this as well. "They were not in the garden?"

"That is an answer I don't know for sure. Some think that when humans ate from the tree they chose different fruits, some ate the apples and were turned out as mere humans while others chose differently and were turned into beasts when they were thrown out; vampires and werewolves. Others think that perhaps they didn't come from the garden at all, that they were already on the earth when the humans arrived and became their prey and their only means of adding to their populations. Earth was a place where god's mistakes had been thrown."

Jonah gave an offended huff.

"I'm not saying I believe that, just what some think. Everyone that old is gone, so we only have vague legends now. Our two species didn't heal entirely, we never really learned to live and work together again outside of the garden. Though there was still breeding, obviously or neither you nor I would be here, it was still all too easy for the vampires and werewolves to take us down to nearly non-existent."

"So our greatest powers are useless against each other, but deadly to the vampires and werewolves, and humans of course?"

"My fangs could do a decent amount of damage, possibly fatal, but it wouldn't be from the venom, no."

"And I am the last webmaker because of some jealousy from the daywalkers about getting kicked out of the garden? So, you asshole daywalkers wouldn't protect us?" Aranha couldn't believe the insanity of that idea. How had they come to this point?

"It certainly added to the problem. I believe that if the

webmakers and daywalkers could have worked together we never would have been taken down to so few in number. There was just too much bad blood. The vampires and werewolves took advantage of our weak moment."

"So why am I going along with all this if you aren't a threat to me?"

Dag gave an exasperated sigh and turned to face her. "Because you care about this world and you know that I'm doing something good for it." He paused and gave a little laugh. "Or maybe it's just morbid curiosity, I don't know. Are you suicidal? Since you're here and not likely to jump out of the moving vehicle... I hope. Let's talk about what might happen when we get to the daywalker compound."

"Like I might be attacked and imprisoned, then fed to a werewolf?"

Jonah growled.

"Definitely not fed to a werewolf," Dag assured them both.

"Well, what a relief," she said sarcastically.

"We have two choices, the way I see it. You two can waltz in beside me, and doubt not that I will do my best to keep you safe." He spoke fiercely and she believed his words. "Or you can hide in the car and we can leave just as soon as possible with no one the wiser until we have the evidence we need about the vampires. Then, if necessary we can reveal your existence, or not."

"Choose your own method of death," she grumbled. "Well how about I shift, sit on your shoulder and make sure you aren't selling us out to your buddies?"

"If you want to risk being found, we may as well walk in with heads high and knives drawn."

She knew he was right, but it killed her to think of hiding in his car while he went in where she would have no idea what he could be negotiating or revealing. She glanced back at Jonah.

Fear filled his face and he was biting his lip nervously. She couldn't risk putting him in danger, or in a situation where he might lose control. "We'll wait."

"Good."

"Just don't forget to leave the windows down, and park in the shade."

He laughed and she glared.

"Sorry, it's just that, that's what you do when you have to leave your dog in the car on a hot day."

"Funny," she grumbled.

About twenty minutes away from the place, she shifted and this time, she didn't bother undressing first. She figured she was better off hiding as a spider and Jonah was so small he could fit on the floorboards of the back seat if he really squished down. It would be difficult for anyone to notice them unless they were really looking.

"Whoa, are you okay in there?" Dag lifted her shirt and moved it aside.

Aranha waved three of her arms at him in what she hoped indicated that not only was she fine, but he should definitely keep back. A misplaced hand could do some serious damage. She'd chosen a sleeker form this time, an elongated abdomen with silver dots.

"You're different," he said with a snicker.

She didn't try to answer, this wasn't Charlotte's Web and he wasn't some dumb pig.

"She can be any kind of spider shape, but always the same colors," Jonah offered as explanation.

"Yeah, I guess I forgot about that. My mother was black and blue. You'll be safe as long as you stay down back there and quiet. If anyone comes up to the car, yell, loud, and I will get here as fast as I can."

"I will kill to protect her," Jonah said fiercely.

"I know," Dag said.

Aranha crawled to a shady spot on the floor and waited, wondering what kind of huge mistake she was making. There had been a few revelations that she wanted time with and this was a great opportunity. Not the least of which, was the fact that she wasn't a mortal danger to daywalkers, and they weren't a mortal danger to her. That was not what her mother had taught her. Her mother had said *all* immortals were a danger to webmakers, including daywalkers before they'd died out. She'd always kind of assumed her mother had killed her father, probably in a passionate frenzy.

So what of the legends of the garden that Dag had spoken of? If that was true, then vampires and werewolves were certainly dangerous, as she'd always known, but daywalkers maybe weren't. Daywalkers should be willing to help remove vampires from power without any other reason, so why was there hesitation? Other than the obvious, that they could kill us. Wasn't immortal death worth risking to free the masses from such a blight?

How many daywalkers remained, she wondered. If their numbers were small, that would explain their hesitation as well. It bothered her that the daywalkers seemed to have accepted the monsters as rulers rather than continued to try and kill them. The monsters had killed off any chance for them to mate and produce children and continue the species, why wasn't that enough motivation?

Whether the vampires and werewolves were created evil, or had chosen the wrong type of apple, most were useless beasts, *and* only able to make more of themselves by killing humans. Wasn't that what Dag had meant? It wasn't until the humans were cast out to earth that the vampires and werewolves were able to increase their numbers. An accident of design by the gods seemed to be unlikely.

Something was missing from the story, she was certain.

Her mind drifted to the fact that daywalkers were only male and webmakers only female, created for each other by some overseeing gods who thought they'd be a perfect match. Then got pissed off when they had their own minds and prejudices. Was she half daywalker, only a webmaker because she'd been born female instead of male... She shook her head and wiggled all eight legs. This was all too much, she'd never been a big believer in religion, but answers were something she'd been seeking since she was sixteen. She'd always thought her mother would tell her everything in time, no rush, they were immortal! But then she'd been gone... too late had come. That was something she never would have predicted.

"I'm pulling into the driveway, the house is a long way off the main road, sorry about the bumps. I'll park under a tree across from the house, you won't be close enough to be scented, and you will be in shade. I can't guarantee how long I'll be in there, but I won't be longer than necessary. Sten probably just wants an update on my life and dealings with the vampires. Sten won't deal with them directly but likes to keep an eye on things from afar. I'll let him know of the strange things I've been noticing, but won't mention you or the webs." He took a deep breath. "If I'm not back by sundown... shift and get the hell out of here, take the car. Don't come in after me and don't hesitate. Retrieve the webs tomorrow and do what you think is best with the information. Just keep in mind, daywalkers aren't supposed to be the enemy." He gazed down at her in the shadow and his voice got a little husky. "We were actually made for each other."

She was glad she couldn't respond in that moment. She wondered what he might be walking into that made him nervous. Part of her wanted to stop him, or go with him as backup. Mostly she wanted to make sure she and Jonah got through this day safely, Jonah was her number one priority.

Dag parked, rolled down the windows, and set the keys in the cup holder. He looked at her and winked, then he was out of the car and she could hear his footsteps fade.

"Dag! How nice of you to grace us with your presence," a male voice called.

CHAPTER EIGHT

Dag walked away from the car with a feeling of dread. He was halfway to the house when he realized he should have hidden her clothes; they were in a pile on the passenger seat. If anyone got close to the car, they would have some serious questions.

Harold stood on the steps of a three story, sprawling, colonial style estate. Long blond hair, blue eyes and golden skin, but that was where the similarities ended between the two. Harold was Sten's lapdog and willing muscle. He wanted nothing more than to please the *king* and soak up the leftover glory. Dag wanted nothing to do with Sten's bullshit, or his court.

"I don't need to kiss Sten's ass every day to find some kind of meaning in my life," Dag shot back. He wasn't afraid of this little asshole.

"Then why are you here?" Harold sneered.

"Because I have information that needs Sten's attention."

"Dag! My man! Good to see you, brother, it's been too long." Lars walked out of the house and hurried down the steps to slap Dag on the back.

Lars was a very tall man, taller than Dag and his long blond hair was shaved into an impressive mohawk that was French braided and hung to his mid back. His eyes were a deep green and half his face was covered in an intricate tattoo. He was a good man, Dag couldn't understand why he chose to stay here, under Sten's thumb.

"Lars! I wish you'd come to the city more often, there are plenty of beautiful women there to pursue."

"Ack, man, you know I can't stand being around all those people. I'd end up slaughtering a few just to get some air! You move out this way, though, and you won't be able to get rid of me."

Dag laughed and slapped his friend on the back, walking with him into the house, ignoring Harold's glare as they passed. Lars sniffed the air and gave Dag a curious look but didn't say anything.

"How can you stand being around that asshole all the time?" Dag grumbled, trying to keep the subject off what he might smell like.

"He's not so bad, once you get over the fact that he's a total kiss ass tattle tale. At least he can drink, and he can fight."

"I guess that counts for something," Dag agreed halfheartedly.

"So, what brings you to our little compound?"

"Sten wanted to see me, and I have some news to share." Dag looked around to make sure no one was close enough to hear. "I think the vampires are up to something, and I should have proof tomorrow."

Lars' eyes narrowed and he moved closer. "I would love to take those bloodsuckers out. You just tell me when, brother, and I am there!"

"Dag!" Sten's voice called from the top of the staircase, stopping any further conversation, which was probably best because

Dag was very close to spilling all of his secrets to his oldest friend.

"Sten, I am sorry it's taken me so long to get here," he lied. "Things have been busy in the city." Dag knew what to say to appease the man, he had to play the game to ensure he could keep living his life the way he wanted without trouble.

"Come on up, we will talk in the library." Sten motioned for Dag, then walked away.

"I'll catch you before I leave," Dag told Lars, then went up the stairs.

He found Sten lounging on a throne surrounded by books he doubted Sten had ever read. He was wearing a silk kimono and matching pants. His blond hair was loose around his shoulders and his dark blue eyes watched Dag carefully. He looked relaxed and soft, but Dag knew better. Sten was ruthless and he was in control of a lot of daywalkers who could potentially rally against Dag at the snap of Sten's manicured fingers.

Dag walked forward and grasped Sten's offered hand, kneeled and kissed his knuckles. He hated it, but he would do what was necessary, especially today.

Sten looked mildly surprised by Dag's pleasantness. "Please, have a seat." Sten pulled his hand away and motioned to a nearby seat. "What news of the big city have you brought us today?"

"There's been movement among the vampires lately. More of them have come to the city and they move about in large groups. I feel like they are planning something, something big and it can't be good."

"Sounds like flimsy evidence, Dag." Sten clicked disapprovingly. "You can't expect me to start a war over a family reunion."

"I don't," Dag said quickly and Sten looked at him sharply. "With all due respect, my king. I only wanted to alert you to the change and assure you that I am digging for more information. If there is something important going on, then you will be able to decide what to do with the information, of course."

"Of course," Sten muttered. He picked up two cigars and held one out to Dag.

Hope of a quick getaway vanished as he accepted the offer. He lit Sten's first, then his own. "Very nice. Cuban?"

"Only the best, I have my vices you know."

"Deserved after so many years, certainly." Dag almost gagged on his own ass kissing. This was why he stayed away. If he had to do this every day, he would end up killing Sten, or Sten would kill him. Once upon a time, his own father was in charge. Sten had been his second in command. They'd gone off on a mission together, only Sten had returned. Dag never got over his doubt about the story Sten returned with. Although it set Dag's father up to look like a hero, it didn't sit well with him. He just didn't think his father could have made a simple stupid sacrifice to save Sten, it didn't make sense. He'd been too young to challenge Sten then, and when he'd been old enough, it hadn't felt necessary, he didn't want Sten's position, he just wanted his own life.

"Harold tells me your bar was closed last night, he was disappointed."

"Yes, I was feeling particularly hungry, so I decided it best to close the bar and find a companion for the night."

"He also said he spotted a feisty looking silver-haired goddess leaving your building. Was that your companion?"

Dag puffed on his cigar to buy time and think. He hadn't expected this, but he should have. Harold probably had been standing outside his building when he'd called. Had he followed Aranha? Did he know what she was?

"Yeah, I brought her home but she got spooked so I let her go and ended up going out for a bite. Found a nice young body to fill my needs." He laughed but he knew it didn't come out quite right.

Sten laughed as well but Dag didn't trust it. "Dag, did I ever tell you about the woman I once loved?"

"No," Dag said with genuine shock, he honestly didn't think Sten had it in him to love anyone but himself.

"I did, I loved deeply once. Come, walk with me." He crushed his cigar in a crystal ashtray and stood.

Dag did the same, unsure where this was going and very glad that he had told Aranha to get out if he didn't return by sundown. If Sten was truly angry that Dag hadn't been to see him and report in a while, this could get dangerous. He'd seen Sten take his anger out on others for minor offenses. Locked them up in chains, away from the sun and starved nearly to death. It wasn't a fate Dag wanted to experience, but he would *not* put Aranha in danger. He'd offered her his shield and although she may not understand what that meant, it didn't change anything in his mind. He was bound to protect her with his life, and he would.

"I don't think I ever told you about my life before I came here, have I?"

"No, I don't believe you have."

Sten started to walk, Dag had no choice but to follow. "I was one of the first earth-born generations." He paused at the library door and turned to look Dag right in the eye. "Did you know that?"

"I had no idea you were that... ancient." Dag settled on the word, fearing old would be offensive.

"Yes, I was born of a webmaker and a daywalker who tried to stay together despite the split that had occurred." He opened the door and continued walking. "It didn't last, my mother was tempted away by a werewolf, dumb beast. She killed him, of course, and then herself because she just couldn't live with the guilt of what she'd done. Destroying our family then killing the one she'd left us for." He stopped at the top of the stairs. "My father would have killed her if she'd not done it herself. I would have done the same," he said without feeling.

Dag glanced down briefly, hoping they were heading out of the house, perhaps Sten was just walking him to the door.

"Do you know what a webmaker must do to kill herself?"

"I have no idea."

"She sacrificed herself to a vampire, she let him feed on her and kill her with his venom." Sten continued on down the long hallway, past door after door without stopping. "It couldn't have been a pleasant death, I'm certain it was neither quick nor painless." There was no emotion in his voice as he talked of his mother's suicide.

A door loomed in the distance at the end of the hall and Dag had a feeling he didn't want to make it there. Not without knowing what Sten was up to.

"What more do you need from me today? I have a plan in place to gather more information about what the vampires are up to. I should be getting back to the city."

Sten didn't miss a step, just kept walking toward the door. "I grieved her, for many years and watched the world grow and change."

Dag wasn't sure if Sten was speaking of his mother or lost love at this point, but it didn't really matter, all that mattered was where he might be leading him.

Sten sighed heavily. "Humans destroying each other, vampires and werewolves destroying the webmakers and daywalkers. Few of us were born, even more dying." He stopped at the door. "You know this part, you were born one of the last. Your own mother and father destroyed by the beasts we now submit to in so many ways, that we cower from. It's an insanity that I am so sick of!"

"Yes, I am doing all I can to figure out their next move. I believe it's coming soon."

"That is good," Sten opened the door. It led to a small stairway going up past the third floor to the attic. Sten mounted the stairs.

Dag followed, being sure the door behind him stayed open. "With your permission I would like to gather enough information to bring to the clan and rally them against the vampires."

"It would take quite an offense to make us risk that. With no real way to perpetuate our species, we are in the position that the vampires and werewolves once were, before the humans arrived," Sten reached the top of the staircase and disappeared into the room, "or so the legend goes."

When Dag got to the top, he was surprised to see it looked much like any other attic, dusty and full of trunks and furniture. A small window looked out onto the back lawn and a bare lightbulb hung from the ceiling. It wasn't a torture chamber.

Sten was kneeling in front of a trunk. He didn't look at Dag, just patted the floor beside him. Dag knelt there next to him.

"I loved once, many years ago. I found a young woman in Portugal." He lifted the lid of the trunk and shuffled through what looked like stacks of cloth and old documents. He pulled out a small box. "I gave her this on the day she told me she was to bear me a child." Sten opened the box and revealed a gold bracelet with turquoise stones.

"It's beautiful," Dag whispered, wondering where the hell this conversation was going, and very afraid he knew.

"She left it behind when she ran with the infant, a girl. There were already daywalkers at our door trying to lay a claim on the child, the last known female, the last chance to carry on our two species. Carinen didn't think I could protect our daughter." He said the last with anger in his voice.

Dag's throat closed. He didn't dare speak.

Sten turned and looked straight into Dag's eyes. "I believe you found her. Did you know what she was when you met her?" His eyes narrowed, accusing.

"I questioned it," he said carefully, still not willing to admit anything, especially in light of this development. Could Sten be Aranha's father?

Sten sighed and turned back to stare at the bracelet. "I find that hard to believe," he said with deadly calm.

Dag felt his whole body go on alert, sure Sten was about to attack.

"The description Harold gave though, it sounds just like Carinen," Sten continued. "I have told my men to find her, whoever brings her to me will have the honor of her hand. We must continue the species."

Dag wanted to explode, she belonged to him! No other could have her! "I will do all I can to find her, my king," he managed to say between clenched teeth.

Sten put the bracelet back in the box, buried it beneath the cloth and shut the trunk lid. "I expect you will. If we can secure the ability to reproduce, we will have the upper hand on the vampires and werewolves. There will be nothing to hold us back. We can finally make things right." He looked at Dag, his blue eyes wide and a little crazed. "We could make this earth our garden. It will be like before and we won't have to hide from humans, they need not fear us. They were created to live with us in harmony—sacrificing as necessary yes—but we were to care for them. Not like the werewolves and vampires do, ruling with fear and striking from shadows." Sten shook his head.

"But we still prey upon them, how could they not fear us? Isn't that what led to dissent in the garden at the beginning?"

Sten frowned, not used to being questioned. "Then we will rule over them, with no one to try and usurp control, nothing will stop us from taking our place as head of the food chain."

The sudden change of tune was not a good sign and the glint in his eyes made Dag catch his breath.

He was crazier than Dag had thought. He was ready to sell his daughter and breed her out, then take an army against their food source. It didn't make sense.

"Have you already sent the others?" Dag asked carefully, trying to keep the concern out of his voice.

"Yes, I sent them first thing this morning. They will be scouring the city as we speak. She will be found and she will be brought here, whether she likes it or not. Harold and Lars chose to stay behind on guard."

Dag could only nod. He needed to get out of here, needed to get Aranha as far from this place as possible, and the city. His mind spun, where would they go? Europe perhaps, he hadn't been in years, and he knew of some nice places they could lay low.

Sten's eyes cleared, he slapped Dag on the back and stood. "So, my boy. I expect you wish to get back to the city and search for yourself. She will be quite a prize for whoever finds her first. Breeding with a webmaker, I can tell you it is something beyond measure. She will be queen and her mate, king!"

"Yes, I must go," Dag agreed heartily.

Sten led the way back down from the attic and to the top of the stairway that led to the first floor. "I leave you to it, my boy. I trust you won't disappoint."

Dag nodded, bent and kissed Sten's knuckles again, then hurried down the stairs. He wanted to speak to Lars but couldn't risk looking for him. When he opened the front door, his eyes locked onto the car across the way, still in the shade, looking just as he'd left it. It felt like he'd been gone hours, so much had occurred, but it couldn't have been more than thirty minutes.

"Dag," Lars' voice stopped him as he started down the front steps.

Dag turned and saw his friend sitting in a chair on the porch. Lars stood and covered the distance between them quickly.

"Lars."

Lars got close and whispered. "Your car smells of her. I watched, Harold looked at it curiously but walked away, I don't think he has any interest in being in charge of breeding a woman."

Dag narrowed his eyes and stiffened, ready to deny, to fight, whatever he had to do. Lars was his friend, his brother by choice, but he would not let him harm Aranha. Or have her, though he didn't go too far down that line of thought.

Lars laughed. "Fear not, brother. I don't know what you're doing, well I have a pretty good idea, but I have no interest in taking what is yours." His eyes darted to the car. "Curious as I am. I only wish to warn you. I don't trust Harold, he may tell Sten what he supposes, choose your next moves carefully. You smell of her too, only faintly. If Sten didn't notice that already, you might be safe enough."

Dag cursed under his breath. "Thank you, brother."

Lars nodded and stepped back. "If you need me, I will be there."

Dag nodded at Lars, then strode down the steps and across the lawn. He slid into the driver's seat, his eyes searching. When he spied her small black and silver form on the floor of the passenger side, he let his breath out on a long sigh. He looked in the back quickly and saw Jonah cowering there.

"We have a problem," he said and started the car. "Stay down," he told Jonah who grunted in response. As he bumped down the long driveway Aranha crawled from her hiding spot up to the seat.

She stared at him from atop her pile of clothes.

"Wait until we're on the main road, just in case."

She gave no indication of understanding and he was tempted to hiss at her, but knew it wouldn't do any good. She was a goddamn spider, what did he expect from her? His eyes darted around as he drove, wondering if they were being followed. Wondering if they would make it to the main road before Harold reported to Sten that he'd smelled something in the car that was suspect. Would Lars do anything to stop them if they tried to come after him? The main road was in sight, Dag was holding his breath, he stepped on the gas, barely pausing before turning out onto the road and gunning it South.

She shifted then, suddenly just there, naked and angry. "What the hell is going on?"

"Your father has put a price on your head."

CHAPTER NINE

Aranha was speechless, she sat there nude and staring at Dag who refused to look at her, and she was sure he wasn't trying to save her modesty. "Explain," she hissed. Jonah sat up and whined, putting a hand on her shoulder. She instinctively reached up and patted it.

"I feel like this conversation deserves a beer. Get dressed and I'll stop up here."

Aranha pulled on her clothes and tried to make sense of what Dag had said, the implications were massive. Jonah could sense her upset and put both arms around the seat to hug her as best he could.

"Can we run away?" he whispered into her ear.

She slid her gaze over to Dag, he was staring forward, pretending he couldn't hear. "Let's hope that doesn't become necessary," she whispered back, watching Dag as she spoke. He relaxed slightly and she wondered if he was tempted by the price on her head.

Dag pulled into a gas station, pumped and went inside.

"What do you think is going on?" Jonah asked when Dag was outside of hearing.

"I don't know, and I don't like it."

"We could run now," he suggested, a little hopeful. "While he's distracted in there."

"No." She couldn't explain it, but she trusted him and something told her this is where they needed to be. Jonah stiffened and sat back at her response, pouting. "Let's hear him out at least, it's best to know what we are dealing with. We don't want to spend our lives on the run, not if we can help it." She'd been doing exactly that, but it felt different when no one knew you existed, it would be harder if they were actively looking for her.

Dag came back out with a six pack of beer and a bag of jerky. She studied his face as he walked back to the car. His forehead was creased and his mouth was turned down, his eyes shifted constantly, watching. He expected trouble and he worried about their ability to handle whatever it was when it came.

He threw the jerky in the back to Jonah and handed her the six pack. "Werewolves have to eat a lot, right? Protein I assume?"

"Oh! Thank you," Jonah said carefully and looked at her as if he needed permission.

Aranha gave a frustrated sigh and nodded her head. Jonah tore open the package and began shoving it into his mouth. He really did need to eat often, though he'd never outwardly complain about hunger, so she sometimes forgot. Dag's thoughtfulness was unexpected.

"Thank you for thinking of him," she said with a genuine smile at Dag. "I forget sometimes that he has to eat."

Dag just grunted and nodded, then started the car. "I know a little place we can pull over and talk."

They drove another few minutes then he pulled off the main road and down to a little river embankment. He grabbed the beer and got out without saying anything. She followed,

Jonah close behind. Dag took a small blanket out of the back of the car and walked down close to the water. It was a really beautiful place, far enough from the main road and with enough trees between to keep the road noise down. Sun shone down on the patch of grass he chose.

He laid the blanket out and sat down, leaned back on one elbow looking relaxed and absolutely sexy as hell. It irritated her that he looked that good, meanwhile she was questioning why her supposedly dead father had put a hit on her!

She cleared her throat and joined him on the blanket, careful not to get too close. "You've been here before?"

"I lived with Sten for a time at the compound there. Not for long, but when I did, this was a close place to find my thoughts when I needed to. Also a good place to energize in the sun." Dag opened two beers and held one out to her and one to Jonah.

Jonah took his and went to sit close to the water with his jerky.

"Thanks." She took a long swig and waited for him to start talking.

"Harold saw you leave my building last night."

"Shit," she whispered.

"Yeah. He reported what he thought he saw back to Sten, of course. What was your mother's name?"

"Carinen."

"Sten claims to have loved her deeply, claims that when she had you, she ran because she was scared of what might happen to you as the last webmaker. The daywalkers were already desperate at that time to find a way to keep their species from going extinct, you would have been courted by everyone." Dag gave a derisive snort. "It only delayed the fact."

"Sten is my father?" Aranha whispered, disbelieving.

"He thinks so," Dag said carefully. "He has sent all of his men out to find you. Whoever comes back with you, will be given the honor of being your mate, in order to keep the species going. He'll be king and you will be queen."

"Queen of what? A floundering species hiding in the shadows, quivering in fear of the vampires and werewolves? No thank you." She concentrated on the least offensive part of what he was telling her while emotions and thoughts swirled wildly inside of her.

"He thinks that he can rally the daywalkers if there is a guaranteed way to keep the species alive. He plans to take control from the vampires. You'll have the new order to rule over if he has his way."

Dag's voice was far too calm. It grated on her nerves. She had no idea what he was feeling about all this, and for some reason it mattered to her.

"While I'm busy breeding his army? Did you sell me out, ready to claim your prize? Do *you* want to be king, Dag?" She couldn't help the accusatory tone.

From where he sat near the water, Jonah eyed them both with wide eyes and an open mouth. He looked like he was ready to run at the first sign of danger. Aranha tried to give him a comforting smile, she wasn't sure it really helped, though, by the fearful look he gave her in return.

Dag lolled his head back and looked straight into her eyes. "I have no interest in a woman who has no interest in me. I have never wanted to be king of anything and I would never sell anyone out to a psychotic man who plans to give his long-lost daughter away as a finder's fee to be bred like a prize-winning mare."

He turned back to stare at the water and Aranha smiled. His answer was absolute perfection, and she believed every word of it. "My mother told me that my father died when she was pregnant."

"She was scared, so she ran. I imagine she didn't want you to search for him at any point."

"Yeah, I suppose so. She also told me that daywalkers were extremely dangerous. I assumed they were going to try and kill me, but using me to breed a world of immortal children is just as bad in some ways. If I had understood better, I never would have begged her to stop running." Guilt welled up inside her, familiar and complete. If she hadn't been desperate for some kind of normal life, they wouldn't have been in one place for long and she never would have revealed herself to a werewolf. "It's my fault they found her," Aranha said softly. "A werewolf followed me home. He came back that night with his vampire master and killed her in front of me."

Dag reached out and touched her arm. She hadn't realized he'd turned to look at her as she'd spoken.

"She died protecting me, her last act was tearing out the bastards throat." Aranha let out a teary laugh, "I ran, sixteen and on my own ever since."

"She died protecting you, giving you a chance to make your life whatever you want it to be."

"Yeah, and look what I've chosen."

"What do you want to do now? That's what's important. I wouldn't blame you if you wanted to run. You could go to Europe, disappear for a century. It will take him a long time to give up searching America. I would hint that you talked about California maybe, I'll keep your secret. Or go with you, help protect you."

Aranha considered his offer, it was certainly what she wanted to do earlier today. What she'd been doing for over two hundred years. Run, hide and make no connections. His blue eyes tugged at her on a deep level, she knew she was probably making a huge mistake and taking unnecessary risks, but she wasn't sure she was living life if she wasn't risking getting a little hurt.

"I can't ignore the fact that the vampires have an innocent human they're holding captive, or that they are up to something." She took a deep breath and smiled what she knew was probably an unconvincing smile. "I have webs to collect, and I plan to get you whatever information you need to go after them."

"You're sure?"

"Yeah, I'm sure."

Jonah whined, no doubt he was voting for a European vacation.

"I think we're going to need backup." Dag pulled out his cell and she scrambled away. Jonah jumped to alert, ready to bolt or attack. "Trust me," Dag said calmly, never breaking eye contact. "You will have to trust me. I swear I won't put you in danger."

She wanted to trust him, so badly. She yearned to let go and trust someone to care for her, to protect her. Jonah wanted to be that for her, but he couldn't, not really. She protected him after all, he was just learning how to be a werewolf and what his strengths were. She never let herself think about her situation enough to care about what she knew she'd never have. Except here Dag was, offering her a hand, and dammit, she wanted to take it. "Okay," she managed to squeak out. She hoped he didn't break the tentative trust. She wasn't sure she would ever try again if he did.

Dag punched a few numbers on his phone and held it up to his ear. "Lars, brother. I need you to meet me. Yes, great." He hung up and smiled. "I hope you don't mind a little romp in the hay," he laughed.

Jonah growled and Aranha glared as images of them rolling around naked filled her mind. She did *not* want to go there with him, that was too complicated. There were even more reasons now than ever to keep those lustful urges at bay, thanks to her father. She had no interest in being the jewel in anyone's crown, or have the responsibility of species resurgence. Maybe the world would be better off if the webmakers and the daywalkers disappeared; after taking out the vampires and most of the werewolves of course.

"I'm only joking, there's an old barn I know, where we can wait out the day and night. Lars will meet us and we can form a plan."

"I hope for your sake, you are," she hissed and finished her beer. "Do we need to go now?" She was enjoying the calm of this place, the running water and singing birds were relaxing. The air was cool as it breezed up off the water and through the dark trees.

"Nope, we can stay as long as you like."

Aranha laid back and let her mind drift until she succumbed to the exhaustion that was suddenly so heavy on her body. Too much had happened and she hadn't slept in far too long. Her dreams were disturbing. Someone was calling to her, begging for help but she couldn't find them. There was a thick fog all around her and she could barely move. She pushed through, swimming in it. Too late, she realized it was smoke and everything around her was burning. Flames began to lick up her legs and she tried to scream, but she only choked on the smoke filling her lungs. Where was Dag, he was supposed to be helping her, guarding her, he had promised to keep her safe!

She woke up screaming and Dag was pulling her into his arms, speaking softly. "It's alright, Aranha, just a dream. You're alright."

She let herself be comforted for a moment, her body still shuddering from the dream. It wasn't unusual for her to have a nightmare, but it was unusual for her to have someone there to comfort her when it was over. His arms were strong and his voice soothing. He stroked her hair gently, surrounding her with his delightful male scent. Soon her heart was beating hard for a different reason and she extricated herself from his lap.

"Sorry about that," she stammered.

"Don't apologize, Aranha, we can't control our dreams."

His voice was still soft and she glanced up at him. His face was concerned and his body was relaxed; but his hands were fisted tightly, as if he were ready to do battle against her imagined enemies. "Should we head to the barn? Lars might be wondering where we are, how long was I asleep?"

"About an hour I think. Seemed like you needed it."

Aranha was a little embarrassed. She couldn't believe she'd fallen asleep out in the open, with a near stranger! That was dangerous.

"Where's Jonah?" She looked around, suddenly worried.

"He went for a walk, I figured it was safe enough, he *is* a predator."

"Yeah, he should be okay," she said, a little unsure. He was a predator who had never really been properly taught. She'd done what she could, but she was no werewolf. "Want to go for a swim before we head to the barn?" she asked, standing quickly and stripping down. He'd already seen her naked so it wasn't that big a deal, she reasoned. She jumped into the icy water and let it wash away her worries.

Dag had watched her sleep, had loved the opportunity to really study her features without her glaring at him for it. She had a very delicate nose, dark lashes and a delightful little mole high on her left cheek. Her mouth was the perfect shape and the color of a ripe strawberry. When she'd started to twitch and groan, he'd been tempted to wake her up but hadn't until she'd cried out his name. He couldn't resist then, he'd pulled her into his arms, aching to destroy the invisible enemy. As her body had settled, he hadn't missed the uptick in her heartbeat. When she'd pulled away it had taken all his self-control not to pull her back in his lap and press his lips against hers.

Now she was naked in the water, tempting him better than any siren ever could. He could see his imminent demise on the horizon and he was ready to rush headlong into it. He stood and undressed, knowing he had nothing to be ashamed of. He went slow enough to be sure she got an eyeful; he felt like a peacock trying to attract a hen as he strode toward the water. Her eyes landed on him and widened, that was it, mission accomplished.

He jumped into the water and dipped under, letting it cool his desire. When he came up for air, she was further away and he couldn't help a low laugh. He disturbed her as much as she did him, and for now, that knowledge was enough.

After a few minutes of cooling down, they headed for the shore, neither breaking the delicate silence. Dag offered her the blanket to dry off but she just shook her head and disappeared. He searched the ground and spotted a black and silver spider scurrying away from the puddle of water left behind. When it reached a dry spot she shifted back, completely dry.

"Now *that* is a nice trick," He used the blanket to dry himself off as she pulled her clothes on.

"It certainly comes in handy every once in a while," she laughed.

Dag pulled on his jeans but didn't bother with the shirt, his long hair would take a bit to dry anyway and there was no reason to let his shirt get soaked in the process. He caught Aranha eyeing him covertly as he folded the blanket and placed it back in the trunk. He didn't want to investigate his motivation too closely, but he knew that he wanted her. She was attractive and fierce, she would make an amazing partner; in bed and life, he was certain.

Jonah returned then, looking happy. Dag had suggested he go shift and run free in the forest for a bit. He'd wanted some time alone with Aranha and he was certain the simpering thing could use a little forced freedom.

"Jonah, did you enjoy your run?" Aranha asked, welcoming him in for a hug.

"Yes, you went swimming? You smell like the water."

"Yes, it was quite delightful."

Jonah eyed Dag skeptically and he smiled at the boy. It didn't bother him that Jonah didn't trust him; it actually made him like the kid more. Jonah obviously cared deeply for Aranha and would do whatever he could to protect her. She needed that even if she would never admit it.

The drive to the barn was quiet and easy, all of them lost in their own thoughts. The barn was a place he and Lars had discovered years ago. An hour from Sten's compound, it had been abandoned but held up pretty well as long as it wasn't raining. It offered a sanctuary for the two and they'd often gone there to clear their heads when Sten's oppressive rule was too much. It should be a safe place to wait until they could retrieve the webs. He'd called Lars in because there seemed to be so much more on the line now and he had no one else he trusted. Aranha's safety was priority number one, whatever the vampires were up to was number two.

The barn was mostly as he remembered, a little taller grass surrounding it and a couple fewer boards still attached. No houses nearby and no sign of anyone having come or gone lately aside from the truck that sat outside. Lars leaned against the tailgate, arms crossed and eyes hidden behind sunglasses. He looked relaxed but Dag knew better, he was always on alert.

"Whoa, is that Lars? He looks like a male model turned wrestle mania star," Aranha gasped.

Dag gripped the steering wheel tighter and glared at his friend. Maybe this was a bad idea. "Yeah, Lars. He doesn't trust anyone so don't do anything that might make him think you're dangerous."

"Do you all look like that?" she whispered.

Dag couldn't help laughing at the awe in her voice. "Basically, yeah, though I would say Lars got all of our best features."

Aranha looked at him quizzically. "Maybe, but your face is softer and I like that." Her face flared red after the words were out. "Not that it matters, I'm sure you both do just fine with the ladies before you sink your fangs in."

"Wouldn't you like to know," he said and let his fangs descend for just a moment as he grinned at her.

She rolled her eyes and turned away, but he could hear her heartbeat quicken and that made him very happy. He parked next to Lars' truck and hopped out, hurrying to open her door. She moved cautiously, eyeing Lars. "Is he going to show me his fangs too," she whispered with a wink.

"Better not," Dag growled.

Jonah hopped out and grabbed Aranha's arm nervously.

"Dag, my brother." Lars said as they approached. He didn't move from his relaxed position. "This is the little thing that's got everyone running around the city with their tongues hanging out?"

Dag laughed, Aranha glared. "I assure you I have no interest in them or their tongues." She held out a hand to shake. "Aranha. You must be Lars. Dag says you're trustworthy but I'm not sure I trust him, so..."

Lars laughed and took her hand. "Smart woman, I like you already. Why is there a wolf with you?"

Jonah was standing behind Aranha, unsure and uncomfortable.

"This is Jonah, he's mine," Aranha said firmly.

"You are mated to a young werewolf!" Lars said with undisguised shock, and a little disgust. "That changes things a bit."

Aranha laughed, "No, more of an adopted son situation. I assure you, he means no one harm and I expect him to be treated well."

"Anything for you, my lady," Lars said with a dramatic bow.

Dag hissed and Lars' eyes shot to him, his lip twitching. "I have some beers to pass the time with while we discuss the plan." Dag said quickly, trying to cover his reaction.

"Perfect," Lars reached into the back of his truck. "Me too!"

"What did you tell Sten?" Dag asked as they headed into the shade of the barn.

"I told him I'd changed my mind about finding the girl, he was happy to hear it and didn't question it."

"Why would anyone not want to have a prisoner for a wife and a kingdom to rule over," Aranha said sarcastically.

They settled inside and cracked open the beer. They discussed the possibilities of what the vampires were up to, coming to no conclusion more nefarious than them drinking blood or trying to turn more humans. Dag was certain it was something bad and he trusted his instincts.

"When have you known the vampires to hold anyone for more than a day or two? That girl was resigned, comfortable and not bitten. There is no way she's just another meal and if they were going to try and turn her, they would have done it already and she'd be dead or turned." Dag argued.

"How do you know she's not now?" Lars countered. "Did you see her there when you went in this morning?" he asked Aranha.

"No," she admitted. "But I agree that something weird is

going on. I am very careful to avoid all immortals in the city and it got very hard recently to stay out of the vampires' way. They haven't been that dense in a city since I don't know when. Never, that I've seen."

"Their little party is tomorrow night?" Lars asked.

"Yep, they will be picking up their meal tonight. Well, their little human servant will be," Aranha sneered.

Lars looked thoughtful. "A human picking up human whores as their blood donors?"

"Yeah, that was what I overheard."

"What if we didn't have to send you in as a spider again. What if you posed as a human and let him pick you up?"

"Their werewolves would sense me."

"Your smell is very distinct and pleasant, I must admit," Lars said with a smile.

Dag bared his teeth at his friend from behind Aranha. He didn't want her to see him being possessive, but he couldn't help warning off Lars and any ideas he might have about her. Lars looked at him and his smile widened.

"Then perhaps our only option is to go in during the day and retrieve the webs. I would say we stake the place out tonight too. It would be good to figure out how many vampires we're dealing with," Lars suggested.

"You're right, the more we can figure out, the better, and with all of the daywalkers in the city searching for Aranha, we shouldn't have anyone bother us."

Aranha turned to look at Dag, her face was guarded. "I will need to eat tonight, I can't risk my energy being low. Shifting so often takes a lot out of me. I have to return to the city."

"Well, fuck," Lars said.

"You didn't eat last night like I told you, did you?" Dag accused.

She bristled. "As if you can *tell* me to do anything, Dag. You aren't in charge of me."

Jonah growled his agreement and Lars shot him a look but only watched, waiting to see if he was a danger.

"No, I'm just the one trying to keep you alive," Dag grumbled. "To the city," he said with a sigh.

CHAPTER TEN

Aranha was kicking herself for not eating last night. After she'd left his condo she hadn't thought it necessary. She could sustain minimal energy on human food and she often went a week or two without draining a kill. If she was going to have to be shifting and fighting, she needed more. She hadn't drained one of her kills in a week and she knew that she wouldn't be at her best if it came to battle.

They'd decided it best to wait out the sun in the barn, she hadn't minded it too much and had even resisted the urge to spin webs and listen in to their thoughts. Lars was a surprisingly pleasant man to be around, calm and level-headed. The jealous way Dag reacted to him was priceless, she had no interest in Lars, but she didn't let Dag know he'd ruined her for the moment on other men. Now she was in the backseat of Lars' truck with Jonah and they were on their way back to the city. The sun was going down, and tensions were high. None of them knew what they might run into. A vampire or werewolf wouldn't be that big a deal, but a whole pack! That might be difficult. If the daywalkers spotted Dag and Lars with Aranha, and if they didn't try and fight to take her for themselves, would they alert Sten to her presence with them? That could be even worse; she wasn't sure she was interested in ever meeting him.

"Where are we going?" Lars asked as they approached the city.

Dag turned and looked at her, raising one eyebrow.

"Perhaps we set up base at your condo. I can go from there on my own." She didn't need them to know all of her secrets, she was also sure that hiding alone would be much easier than hiding with these two hulking men and a skittish werewolf.

"Ha," Dag laughed. "I am not letting you out of my sight. We will go to your kill, then we can wait out the night at my condo and head to the vampire compound before dawn, try to get a head count."

"I don't need bodyguards."

"You didn't need them when no one knew you existed. Now you're on far too many dangerous radars."

"He's right," Jonah whispered.

Aranha rolled her eyes but agreed. If he wanted to witness the horror of what she was, fine. Then maybe he'd stop treating her like she couldn't take care of herself. She directed them through the city to a neighborhood where she knew she had a meal ready for her.

"Park in the next alley."

"This isn't where you left Frank," Dag pointed out.

"No, Frank isn't ready yet," she murmured.

"Who's Frank?" Lars asked as he parked in a narrow alley between two abandoned brick buildings.

"A serial killer who liked to hang out at Dag's bar."

"You let a serial killer just hang out at your place? Was he picking off your customers?"

"I think serial killer is a strong word," Dag said with a huff.

"I know he killed at least one girl he met at your place and was planning to do the same to me. Close enough to a serial killer in my opinion." Aranha was happy to point out.

"Do you always go after serial killers?" Lars turned in his seat and looked at her with a wide smile. "I envy your ability to make noble kills."

"Thank you," she smiled back.

"Let's do this," Dag hissed and opened the door, slamming it shut behind him.

"Your friend is quite the charmer," Aranha said to Lars.

"I think you have him twisted up and he doesn't know what he wants anymore," Lars said with a laugh.

Dag opened the back door. "Are you coming?"

"I'll wait here with the boy, I don't want anyone to steal my truck," Lars said with a smirk.

"You weren't invited," Dag hissed.

"Neither of you need to accompany me," Aranha pointed out, even though she doubted it would stop Dag.

"I'm coming," Dag said in a tone that left no room for argument.

Aranha gave Jonah a comforting look then slipped out of the truck and sauntered past Dag. She walked halfway down the alley, then up a flight of fire escape stairs to a balcony on the second floor. She collected a couple webs along the way and did a quick sweep of thoughts and memories to make sure that no one had come up this way since she'd left. "Hello lovelies," she said to the many spiders she passed along the way.

"Friends of yours?" Dag asked sarcastically.

"Spiders are simple creatures, they just want to eat and fuck."

"I might be a spider," Dag said with a laugh.

Aranha rolled her eyes at the door, and shooed the spiders away who she'd set to guarding it when she'd left. "He was stalking a child," she said as she opened the door. "I caught what he was planning to do. Thank god it was a thought and not a memory." She turned to look straight into Dag's eyes. "I felt no misgivings about what I did to him, he was a monster."

"I wouldn't have either." His voice was serious and his eyes sincere.

"I don't think he ever committed a crime." Aranha wanted to be sure Dag understood. She wasn't out there picking off serial killers all the time. It wasn't all about punishment *after* a crime. If she could prevent harm, she did, without a second thought.

"But he would have, you saved a child." His eyes never left hers, he stepped closer and grabbed her shoulders. "Aranha, I don't believe you kill without reason." His eyes dipped to her lips and his fangs ran out. "I could taste your soul, you know. The blood doesn't lie."

"What did my blood tell you?" she asked, her mouth dry and her throat tight.

"That your intentions are pure. You don't act without cause or reason and you must be made of a little bit of magic because the taste of your blood," he paused and made a sound so deep it must have been a growl, "your blood tasted like heaven."

"Pure intentions, I certainly like to think so," she said, a little breathless.

His eyes met hers again and he leaned in, pressing their lips together in a gentle, searching kiss. He wasn't demanding and she let him probe, let him taste. Her own fangs ran out and she couldn't stop herself from responding to his kiss.

When she did, he crushed her body to his and forced her lips apart, probing deeper, nipping her slightly with his fangs, but she didn't care. She knew he was no danger to her body... her heart and mind were other matters. Everywhere their bodies touched, fires started to burn, slowly taking her over. Her hands ran up his back, fingers searching for the lines of muscle she knew were there, delighting in the feel of his solid form, his nearly unbreakable body. She wouldn't have to hold back, she wouldn't have to worry about a slip on her part ending his life. Her natural instincts, her carnal wishes, she could have them all and he would survive. The thought overwhelmed her and before she could stop herself, she was hopping up and wrapping her legs around his waist. He caught her easily and walked into the building, turning and pushing her against a wall. His mouth moved to her neck and she moaned as shivers ran down her spine. She gripped his hair, holding his mouth against her flesh. It had been too long since she'd allowed herself even a portion of this.

A loud crash in the alley stopped them both. They froze, eyes locked as they listened. "Dag!" Lars yelled and there was another crash.

"Fuck," Dag hissed and stepped away, dropping her gently. "Eat. I'll help Lars. Stay out of sight."

With those demands, he was gone and she was alone, gasping in the dark, knees weak and head spinning. "What the fuck just happened," she whispered.

Still woozy and swaying a little, she walked to her pod. The man was wrapped up in so much web he looked like a giant cotton ball. She sank her fangs through the web and into flesh, drawing out the fluid that his insides had become. She drank until she was full, until she knew she'd be at her best. Full strength and abilities. She would not be a liability, no matter what happened next. She would come back and dispose of what was left another time. The shell of the human would need to be hidden, she knew how to dispose of it so no one would ever come across it.

She peered out the door carefully, not because Dag had told her to stay out of sight, but because she had no interest in being caught off guard. She saw Dag and Lars standing at the back of the truck looking down into the bed at something thrashing around. Jonah was off to the side watching curiously. No one looked harmed.

It seemed safe enough, so she walked down, choosing to go onto the side of the truck where Lars and Jonah stood. She wasn't sure what was between her and Dag, but she didn't want to find out right now.

"What did you catch?" she asked as casually as she could manage, peering down at a large man with a bag over his head. "And why is it still alive?"

"Daywalker. He's our brother, we can't kill him, we just have to keep him from ratting us out," Lars explained.

"Makes sense."

"Did you eat?" Dag asked.

She refused to look at him, just stared down at the body. "Yep. I wouldn't mind some clean clothes, maybe we can head around the corner to my apartment before we go to your swank condo?"

"Speaking of swank, how do you expect to keep this guy quiet long enough to get up the elevator? Your place isn't exactly private or full of the type of people who would look away from such an obvious crime," Lars added.

"We'll take him up the service elevator." Dag's gaze didn't leave Aranha as he spoke, they narrowed on her and it took everything she had not to meet his gaze as she felt it boring into her.

"No one will want to notice a body in the back of your truck in my neighborhood, so no worries there. It's just up the street."

"You've got to be a badass to survive around here," Lars said with a laugh and opened the back door of the truck for her and Jonah.

"It's helpful for storing dead bodies." She smiled and slid into the back of the truck beside Jonah.

Dag hopped into the front and slammed his door.

"Hey, don't break the truck," Lars said playfully, gaining a glare from Dag.

Aranha directed them down a couple blocks and around a corner. They stopped at a small apartment building with a pool that looked like it hadn't been functional in a decade or two. Aranha knew it was a dump, but she didn't care. She didn't pick places to live that were warm and welcoming, she wanted to live where it was dark and safe. Where neighbors avoided knowing you and the rent was cheap. She hated that she felt a tinge of embarrassment having Dag see it.

"Nice place," Lars said sarcastically.

"Yeah, well, it's home for Jonah and I," she laughed. "I'll be right back." She hopped out quickly, Jonah right behind her.

Dag followed. "Not letting you go alone, remember the point is to keep you alive."

She motioned to Jonah. "Not alone."

"He barely counts, he's a child."

"I assure you he can do some damage, and he is very protective."

"I'm coming with you," he said simply.

Aranha frowned but didn't argue further, she knew it wouldn't do any good. He followed them up a flight of stairs, to the end of the landing, and to a door marked 16B. "Hope you don't mind dark and destitute," she grumbled as she opened the door.

She didn't let embarrassment show as she walked into the sparsely furnished living room. She didn't turn to see his reaction, just walked into the one bedroom and started grabbing a few things, Jonah following suit. She hurried into the bathroom to grab a few essentials and caught site of Dag's face. He looked somewhere between shocked and pissed off.

"Ready," she said as she came out of the bathroom, bag in hand.

"You two live like this?"

She put her hands on her hips and gave him a sardonic look. "Like what? Like we might have to pack up and leave at any second? Like we can't bring anyone home for fear of eating them for breakfast? Like we don't have a job and can only afford what we can steal? What did you expect, Dag? I'm not a daywalker trying to pretend I'm human. I'm a fucking webmaker trying not to be discovered or killed!"

"I am *not* trying to be human," he hissed.

"Maybe not, but you don't have to move around constantly either." Her voice cracked a little and she could have screamed she was so mad at herself. Pity, from him or herself, was *not* allowed.

He stepped forward as if he were going to offer comfort.

She stepped back and held up a hand. "No, let's go." She pushed past him and shoved the bags at Jonah, pushing him out the front door, not bothering to wait for anything else from Dag. Jonah hurried in front of her, wanting to get away from Dag no doubt. Aranha heard Dag pounding down the steps behind her. At the bottom he grabbed her arm and forced her to face him.

"You don't have to run anymore, I will protect you," he said fiercely.

His words threatened to warm her and she didn't like it, didn't want to like it. "I don't need protection," she hissed.

"You don't *want* to need it, but unless you want to end up locked in a room with a daywalker husband, I think you *do* need it. Jonah too, he can't be thriving here like this."

She latched onto what she could most deny about his statement. "So you can be that husband who locks me up? No thanks. Jonah and I are doing just fine."

His grip tightened on her arm. "You know that's not what I meant."

She let her fangs slip out, "Let go of me."

He pulled her against him, his eyes were on fire with emotions that she didn't want to reflect. "Not until you admit that I'm the better option. I can keep you safe."

"Don't need it," she hissed trying to pull out of his grasp.

"Everything alright?" Lars said, suddenly right behind her.

He'd moved so fast and quiet that she hadn't noticed, and that scared her.

"It's fine, Lars, mind your own," Dag hissed.

"Brother," Lars said carefully. "Let her go."

Dag broke eye contact with Aranha, his eyes shifting over to Lars. Aranha felt Lars' hand land on her shoulder. She was sandwiched between these two men and Dag looked like he was about to kill someone. He let go of her arm and stalked off to the truck.

Aranha let out a breath then pulled away from Lars and turned to face him. "Your friend is pushy."

Jonah was whimpering and bouncing from foot to foot behind Lars, obviously not sure what to do or who was a threat.

"I won't let him do anything he'll regret, he's not acting himself right now," Lars said reassuringly.

"He's been a grumpy ass since I met him."

Lars laughed, "Okay, maybe he *is* acting himself, but I still won't let him do anything he'll regret."

They walked to the truck where Jonah picked up the bags he'd dropped there. He was looking like he wanted to cry. She gave him a smile and patted his cheek. "It's fine," she whispered and got in the truck.

Dag turned to stare her down in the backseat, his blue eyes blazed with restraint. "I'm sorry," he hissed. "Is your arm alright?"

She touched where there would certainly be a bruise. "Fine," she mumbled.

He huffed and turned around as Lars pulled out and headed toward the better part of town.

Dag's hands were fisted so hard his nails were digging into his palms, the pain kept his mind off the frustrating woman in the backseat. The kiss they'd shared was something he'd never experienced. His life had been full of women, all kinds of women; even a vampire woman once, but that kiss! It touched his soul.

He should have waited, shouldn't have let the moment take him. It was too much for her and he'd scared her. She was so far into denial now; he might have fucked them both, and not in the good way. Then seeing where she'd been living, *how* she'd been living. It killed him to think of her like that. She had no one except a werewolf who was scared of his own damn shadow. They had nothing that wasn't absolutely necessary and lived in a constant state of fear and guard.

He wanted to take it all away, wanted her to give in to him and his ability to protect her. She would need nothing else, no running, no worrying. He could give that to her. He would even take in the boy, offer him protection and training, make him into some sort of a man if he could.

She didn't want it, she was trying to make that very clear and it pissed him off.

He slid his gaze to Lars and his hand fisted tighter. What if she wanted him? *Kill him.* His mind shouted.

He slammed his eyes closed and tried to just breathe. Lars was probably the only daywalker he didn't have to worry about. Lars would never try and take a woman from him. They were brothers by choice and clan, they watched out for each other like none of the others did. They'd made a pact three hundred years ago and it stood.

Dag wasn't used to a woman not falling over herself to get with him, didn't know how to go about wooing her. Had never cared to want to. He let himself briefly entertain the idea of presenting her to Sten and taking her as his prize, just so no one else could have her. He knew it would never work, she'd hate him, probably try to kill him and then definitely run away. He didn't want her by force, he wanted her by choice.

He was so deep into his thoughts that he didn't realize they had made it to his building until Lars cleared his throat loudly to get his attention. "Go around back, skip the garage. We can load him up the service elevator."

Dag hopped out as soon as the truck stopped, anxious to get moving and doing anything to take his mind off Aranha. "Jeb, you don't fight back, and I won't knock you out, deal?" he said to the body.

A grunt was his only reply.

"I'll grab the feet," Lars offered as he came around the side, followed by Aranha and Jonah.

"Great, Aranha you can open the door there and call the elevator down," Dag directed.

Aranha walked off, Jonah following with their bags. Dag grabbed Jeb around the shoulders and Lars got his feet. They'd both known Jeb for at least three hundred years, he was an alright guy, great in a fight and fun to drink with. Dag never would have expected him to get so into this idea of having a wife and being king, breeding more of their species. The bastard didn't even know what Aranha looked like! For all Jeb knew, Aranha was a hideous beast. Dag smiled, she was far from it. His smile faded as he realized how desperate the daywalkers might get if they found out she was a beautiful delicate creature with a passion for life and blood that tasted so good that a drop rivaled the best sex he'd ever had.

"You're growling," Lars said as they rounded the back of the truck and headed toward the building.

"Yeah," he said, not caring to explain.

"If you hold her tight, you will lose her faster than you can even imagine," Lars warned.

"Fuck you, Lars, when did you become mister relationship expert."

Lars laughed. "I know a few things about women, and that one, she'll spook easy."

Dag just grunted in response. He knew Lars was right, but that didn't solve any of the problems that were facing him.

CHAPTER ELEVEN

Dag and Lars got their captive up in the elevator without issue and into Dag's penthouse apartment; he really didn't seem to be fighting them much at all. They dropped him into the corner of the guest bedroom and shut the door. "He'll be fine there for now," Dag said.

Aranha settled into a comfortable chair with Jonah at her feet. She was always a little sleepy after eating a big meal, but she also felt particularly in need of a shower. "Mind if I shower?"

"Not at all, use the one in there." Dag pointed toward a door open to what looked like the master bedroom, then moved to the kitchen and pulled a couple beers out of the fridge. "There's some food in here, Jonah, not much but I keep a few things on hand. We can order some delivery, too."

Jonah looked at her, questioningly. She gave him a smile and nod, then grabbed her bag. Jonah slunk into the kitchen to investigate.

Aranha walked through Dag's bedroom. She wasn't surprised at all to see a bed big enough for three hulking men, covered in black bedding. The walls were a dark grey color and the furniture was rich dark wood. Everything was neatly put away and clean. This was Dag, dark and comfortable. The contrast to her own living quarters was astonishing and she was struck by the unfairness of it all. She'd lived a life on the run, alone and, she could admit to herself, scared. The daywalkers had been hunted too, but they had survived, thrived even. The daywalkers had each other and they had lives to live. Why were the webmakers not given that same chance? What had really happened all those years ago? Was it because they were female? Had that played into their ultimate extinction? She couldn't accept that, she knew she could take on a vampire or werewolf one on one just as easily as a Dag or Lars could. It didn't make sense, and she hated that she may never know.

She hurried into the bathroom and locked the door behind her. Emotions she didn't want were welling up and if Dag offered to comfort her again she thought she just might pull a knife on him.

She took a long time in the shower. It felt so good to stand under hot water that wasn't coming out of rusty pipes. It soothed her as it seared her skin delightfully. When she finally felt her iron control lock back into place, she got out of the shower. She dressed comfortably in black yoga pants and an oversize t-shirt. This was basically a platonic sleepover and she didn't care if she looked cute. She combed out her long hair and left it loose to dry. No use for makeup but she did brush her teeth and was feeling good about herself when she walked out.

She found Dag sitting alone on the balcony, no sign of Lars or Jonah. "Thanks for letting me use your shower. What happened to Jonah and Lars?"

"Jonah is sleeping in the guest room, sort of a guard in case Jeb decides to try and escape, although I tied him up good, so I'm not really concerned. Lars went out for a bite." Dag gave her a sly smile.

"Funny, do you need to do the same? I'm fine here by myself. Unless you don't trust me to not snoop in your underwear drawer."

He looked at her and raised an eyebrow. "Sweetie if you wanted to see my underwear, all you had to do was ask."

"I've already seen them, remember? Black and tight, very nice," she teased.

He stood and they were so close she could feel his breath on her cheek. His eyes were swirling blue now, darker than before. He reached up and touched her cheek, trailing his finger down her neck and around her throat, then straight down between her breasts. When he reached her belly button his hands grasped her waist and pulled her to him.

She was breathless, she knew this was a bad idea. She put a hand to his chest, not pushing him away but stopping him nonetheless. "Dag," she whispered.

"Aranha?"

"I don't think this is a very good idea, there is so much going on right now, I—I just don't..." she trailed off, not really sure what she was trying to say but she knew that them sleeping together was not going to help the situation. She didn't want him to get any ideas about being king with her happily by his side pumping out babies.

He sighed and stepped away, letting his hands drop. "No pressure, just offering you a good way to pass the time. How about a beer instead?"

"Sure," she huffed, more than a little offended by how easily he was taking her rejection. It certainly hadn't felt casual when they kissed. Or the way he'd acted so jealous of Lars. Or how he'd wanted to comfort her in her apartment! "What the hell?" she exploded at his back as he reached into the refrigerator.

He turned quickly, eyes scanning for what upset her. "What is it?"

"Where the hell do you get off acting like you just wanted a quick romp in the hay, no big deal if you don't get it?" she demanded.

A broad smile broke out on his face and he closed the fridge, then handed her the beer. "Are you upset that I am not falling all over myself to have you?"

"No," she lied.

"Do you want me to grab you and kiss you until you can't even breathe, then sweep you off your feet and carry you into the other room?" He spoke slowly and seductively, his eyes boring into her soul as he spoke.

"No," she lied again.

"Because have no doubt, that is exactly what I want to do, I just refuse to coerce or beg. So I guess until you are ready to admit you want me as much as I want you, we are at an impasse."

He walked away and went back to his spot on the balcony. She was left with confusion, but at least she was reassured that he was attracted to her, that was something. She took her beer to a comfortable seat in the living room and curled up, exhausted. Two sips was all she got before she was asleep.

Some time later she was lifted into his arms, she woke up enough to pretend a protest, which he ignored.

"You should be sleeping in a bed."

"Sounds good, sleep's good," she said with a sigh as he set her gently onto the softest mattress she'd ever encountered. She rolled over; she wouldn't turn down some time in this heavenly resting place. She only startled slightly when she felt his weight join her on the other side, but he didn't touch her, didn't move close, so she let it slide. Sleep was too tempting.

The moon was still bright in the sky when Aranha felt his lips touch hers lightly, bringing her out of a very pleasant dream, starring him.

"It's time for us to spy on some vampires, darling."

Aranha opened her eyes and looked at Dag's face just inches from hers. She wanted to reach up and pull his head down, wanted to roll over and let their bodies touch; she wanted to pretend there was nothing in the world more important than them and this bed, in this moment. She settled on safety. "I like your bed."

"I do too," he said with a wink that made her stomach flutter. "It's particularly enjoyable right now."

She bit her lip to keep from kissing him. He moved away with a sigh. "I suppose we had better get a move on. I'm sure we'll have to shake Lars awake out there."

"Poor guy, did he have to sleep on the couch?"

"I'm not sure, he wasn't back yet when I decided to take mercy on you, twisted up and asleep in the chair."

She blushed, "Thanks."

"Any time." He gave her a wide smile, letting her see his fangs were slightly extended and she shivered a little at the sight.

She wondered what it would be like to let him bite her. When he'd licked the blood from her leg wound she'd nearly lost her mind with the sensation. Actually letting him feed deep from her, that would be an experience she was sure to never forget.

He jumped out of bed and she noticed he was wearing only a pair of tight black boxers. His body was male perfection. Muscles bulged and moved as he slid on a pair of shorts and t-shirt. She watched as he pulled on socks and shoes, not embarrassed by her obvious perusal. They'd seen each other naked at the river, but this was different, this was somehow far more intimate. Watching someone get dressed in their bedroom was something couples did, it was personal. He walked into the bathroom and she watched as he braided his hair in one long

French braid. She loved the effect of the shaved sides with the braid, he looked fierce, he was a warrior.

She thought about that first night, which seemed like so long ago—was that really only a day and a half ago?—when he had offered her his shield. How he had pledged to keep her safe. Would he really? She looked around his bedroom, full of things he'd collected over so many years on earth, how long could he keep her?

"You want breakfast in bed, darling?" he asked with a hint of sarcasm.

"I'm getting up," she groaned, "your bed is dangerously comfortable."

"You're definitely in danger if you continue to lay there," he winked and left the room.

She scrambled out of bed when she heard a hissed, "Fuck," from the other room.

"What is it?" she rushed out into the living room as he was coming out of the guest room.

"Lars isn't here." Dag's face was creased with worry.

"Maybe he got lucky?"

"Lars would never skip out on a mission."

"Maybe he slept in his truck?"

"Maybe, you get ready and I'll go look."

Dag left the condo and Aranha hurried to the bathroom. She changed into shorts and a tank top then braided her hair in two French braids and applied a little eye makeup. When she left Dag's bedroom, Jonah was happily sitting in front of the television.

"Good morning, sweetheart," she said, giving him a kiss on top of his head.

"Morning," he said cheerily.

"How did you sleep?"

"Pretty good..." he said carefully.

She forced his eyes to meet hers and raised an eyebrow. "What?"

"I missed you, you were so far away and you were, you were with... with *him*," he whispered and his eyes darted around nervously.

She smiled. "I missed hearing you snore beside me," she teased and he smiled back, but it didn't reach his eyes.

"I don't snore all the time! I will do better," he said sadly.

"Jonah, I was joking."

"But you slept well, with him?"

"I slept well, his bed is comfortable but I didn't sleep *with* him and even if I did it's none of your business," she scolded.

His look of complete degradation made her heart sink. "Sorry."

"What are you so worried about?" she asked, exasperated.

He tried to look away but she forced him to keep her eye contact. "If you love him, you'll forget about me."

She sighed and crouched down so she could look at him on level. "I could never forget about you, no matter who else might come along."

His face brightened a bit. "I could be okay to spend some time here," he said happily.

She laughed, "Yeah, it's a nice place but don't get comfortable, I am not sleeping with him just so you can watch cable."

Dag rushed back in then with a look of murder on his face.

"Oh my god, what is it? Is Lars okay?" Aranha rushed forward but stopped just before touching him, she didn't feel comfortable enough to reach out and try to comfort him, especially when he looked like he was ready to smash a hole in the next thing that slightly bothered him.

He shoved a piece of paper at her. "They've taken him."

"Who?" she asked as she read the letter and gasped.

Your presence has been requested by Quentin Russell at sunset.

"That was in Lars' truck," Dag explained.

"Quentin is?"

"The vampire in charge in this area. He must have taken Lars last night."

"But why?"

"Could be that he just wanted to make sure I showed up to witness whatever they are planning, or..." He looked at Aranha, his eyes full of concern.

"Or?" she prodded.

"Or he knows about you and he wants the chance to eliminate you."

Aranha felt icy fear fill her veins, the urge to run was stronger than ever. Jonah whined and came up close to her, grabbing her arm. She didn't need to be here, she wasn't bound to Lars or Dag. She had a responsibility to keep herself and Jonah alive, no one else, and that was how she liked it. "Dammit," she hissed. "We better get the webs and see what they're planning." She couldn't just run, she needed to know if what they were up to was worth staying and fighting against.

"It's too dangerous, if they already found them, they'll be expecting you," Dag pointed out.

"If they already knew, they would have come up here last night and tried to take me out. They wouldn't be inviting you to a party." She doubted her own words as she spoke, but she was trying to convince herself too. She could at least do this one last thing to help, she didn't have to stick around after that. Lars didn't deserve to be abandoned to the vampires though, no one did. Especially not an innocent young human girl.

"We need Jeb on our side. I don't know how he'll react to being faced with you. He was on your trail when he found us."

"Aspirations of greatness?"

"Something like that, yeah."

"And you don't think he'll be taking a *no thank you* as answer?"

"I think the safest option is for him, and everyone else, to believe that I found you first and you've agreed to be mine."

"You want to be my king, Dag?" she said with more than a little hostility.

"No, I want you to remain safe and this might just be the only way," he hissed.

"I could just as easily say I'm committed to Lars, couldn't I?"

"Good luck with that, he isn't here to defend you. Jeb and anyone else we run across will see you as fair game."

"Oh, how convenient that I'm left with no other option than to let *you* own me!"

"Dammit, Aranha, I am trying to save your ass."

"Yeah," she said carefully. "Save it, I understand."

They glared at each other for a full minute, neither willing to say the things that would make the situation better. Jonah was nervous, his fingers bit into Aranha's arm and he hid behind her, peeking out at Dag and whining every once in a while.

Dag stalked off to the guest room after a moment and came back with their captive, Jeb. He wasn't wearing a bag over his head anymore, but he was still bound and gagged. He looked much like Dag and Lars, tall, muscular and blond, but his hair was cut short into a mohawk and his eyes were a bright green.

"Jeb, this is Aranha, Sten's daughter. She is taken, I found her first and that's that. Now, I can't leave you tied up because I need you to rally the others and meet me at the compound. Lars has been captured and the vampires are planning something nefarious for tonight."

Jeb grunted, his eyes looked her up and down, settling on her chest. She didn't like it and was a little glad Dag had claimed her, at least in Jeb's eyes.

Dag untied Jeb's gag first.

"You are a fucking sight! I can feel my mating instincts kicking in just looking at you. Damn, girl!"

Dag punched him, hard, and he fell to the floor, eyes rolling back in his head.

Jonah laughed and clapped.

"Was that really necessary?" Aranha asked with a laugh.

"I would never allow anyone to talk to my woman that way. If he is going to take me seriously, I have to act accordingly. It would help if you did too."

"Whatever the fuck that means," Aranha grumbled.

"Pretend you like me, shouldn't be that hard." He winked at her. "Think about it the way you treated your last boyfriend."

"I ate him," she said with a straight face and no inflection to her tone.

Jonah nodded furiously in agreement. Aranha loved him for the support, even though he had no idea if it was true or not.

Dag laughed and bent to untie Jeb. "Wake up, brother, I need you to find everyone else who's out here searching. Let them know it's game over and we are on high alert for the vampires. Lars is in danger, Aranha and I are going to go in for more information, then we will meet everyone at the compound."

"Sure," Jeb mumbled as Dag untied him. When his hands were free, he rubbed his jaw. "Damn, man. You better relax because that female is about to cause a whole hell of a disruption at the compound."

"I know," Dag hissed and looked at Aranha.

Aranha didn't respond, she had nothing to say. She wanted to ask why this was her problem, but she knew. Unless she just up and left, which was nearly impossible at this point, she was in this thing, and she seriously doubted she would find any daywalker who was as easy going and reasonable as Dag seemed to be. If she wasn't careful, she'd end up locked in some basement, married to an asshole, instead of just maybe pretending to date one.

Dag let Jeb untie his own feet, then escorted him to the door, shutting it soundly behind him. Before he left, Jeb shot Aranha one last look and there was something very disturbing there.

"Are you sure this is a good idea, that they all know I've been found?"

"Yeah, they know *I* found you. It's over."

"And if they don't agree?"

Dag rolled his eyes. "Are you doubting my ability to keep you safe?"

"From a hundred men who look like they work out as much as you? Yeah, I am."

"We have a pretty strict code; we are clan brothers. We don't take from each other."

She wasn't convinced, partially because she couldn't relate in the slightest, she'd always been for herself. "We'd better go if we plan to try and spy on the vampires before sunrise," Aranha said, not wanting to talk about anything else that needed discussing.

Dag's eyes narrowed slightly but he didn't press her. "I think we should wait."

"Wait?"

"I don't think it's smart to go in before the vampires have gone to bed for the day. They might be expecting that. Who knows what they already know, and it seems we are going in to party tonight anyway, so why worry about getting numbers? I think we wait and go at sunrise, same as yesterday."

Aranha couldn't argue with the logic, and it meant they could spend another couple of hours relaxing here, safe. "Okay, but I get the remote," Aranha grabbed it and threw herself in the chair she'd slept in last night. Jonah settled at her feet and Dag took another chair, watching her more than the television.

The hours were peaceful and comfortable. They watched old horror movies and Jonah ate everything Dag had in his kitchen. It was an odd feeling, like they were playing house, but it wasn't going to last. When the first rays of sunlight were peeking over the horizon, they got ready to go. They were going to invade the vampires' home, then go to the daywalker compound and proclaim a fake relationship. She *was* curious to meet her father, despite the fact that he wanted to give her to one of his men as a prize and expected her to start popping out babies to save their species. It was her own little horror movie.

"We are taking Lars' truck, I assume."

"Yeah, luckily Lars left his keys in the ignition, otherwise I'd be hotwiring the thing."

"You're a man of many talents," Aranha laughed.

"You have no idea," he said, and his eyes dipped down, caressing her from head to toe, leaving no doubt about where he thought his abilities lay.

"Alright, Don Juan, let's go," she said with a voice that was more shaky than dismissive like she'd intended.

As they made their way out of the city she had a sinking feeling that her life would never be the same. She wasn't sure how she felt about that. She looked over at Dag's exquisite profile, she wondered what he really thought about all this. She knew he would fuck her, that wasn't a question, but how far would he go to keep her from being married off to one of his daywalker brothers against her will? And how far would she go?

CHAPTER TWELVE

The drive to Quentin's compound was mostly silent, everyone deep in thought.

Their plan went much like it had the morning before. She undressed, shifted and waited on the door. When the delivery truck passed, they followed. She let out her string and just as she was getting caught by the wind, she heard Dag.

"Be careful," he hissed.

If she could have smiled in her spider form, she would have. He cared and she couldn't help that she liked that. She was pretty sure the last time she'd flown out the window to catch this same delivery truck, he'd only cared about the information she might get, she was a means to an end; but now, maybe more?

She landed on the roof this time and it wasn't as easy to hold on as it rumbled down the driveway. She almost slipped, but got enough web out just in time to stick in place. Stranded between the gate and the house would be the worst of all options she could imagine. Looking back, she saw the same bald angry werewolf at the gate and he was looking at the truck as it went. She wondered if he smelled her again. If the daywalkers all knew about her... did the vampires? What were the chances that the vampires had an informant among the daywalkers?

Fear iced through her as the delivery truck turned and backed up to the kitchen door. Should she hide, or should she do the job she came to do? If she hid, she might save her own ass, if she collected the webs... she might save a girl and who knows how many human prostitutes.

With a hiss she scrambled off the truck when it stopped. She wasn't going to put her life above those innocents she could possibly help.

"Ben, I hope you had a successful night." Billy, the red-haired werewolf called as he stepped out of the kitchen followed by the same blond haired one she'd seen with him yesterday.

"Morning, Billy, Chad." Ben grumbled as he walked to the back of the truck and opened it up.

"You got four! Good job, now we don't have to remind you who's in charge around here," Billy laughed. Ben flinched as Billy reached out to slug him on the shoulder. "Are you and Jane coming to the party tonight?"

"I think we'll pass." Ben's voice shook a little. Aranha felt sorry for the guy, but he *was* bringing women to their death, so she didn't feel *that* bad for him. In fact, he would be a candidate for her next meal.

Billy and Chad laughed heartily at Ben's discomfort and Aranha scurried into the kitchen. They would start unloading the four women and the boxes. It would be just enough time to gather the information from the webs.

The first one she'd left under the kitchen counter. But when she got there, nothing. *Fuck!* What if they'd discovered it, would they know what it was?

Chad walked by with a passed-out prostitute over his shoulder.

"Don't take her downstairs! That daywalker is tied up down

there, but I don't trust him, he could drain these girls; then we'd be screwed for the party tonight," Billy called out.

"Yeah, yeah," Chad grumbled and headed down the hallway.

Aranha hurried to follow. The web she'd left under a table there was still intact. She crawled onto it and let everything it had captured flow into her, she sifted through the thoughts and memories, letting the useless back out and holding onto what might be useful. She let go of party plans, feeding and sex memories, hatred and jealousy; none of that was surprising or useful. She caught thoughts about the captive, Lars. They planned to include him in some kind of ceremony. The party tonight was more than a party, it was something... ritualistic. She couldn't get a clear reading, but it was definitely significant and had something to do with the girl... Evelyn?

Chad passed with the second prostitute and Aranha hurried to the office where she'd left the third web. Thankfully it was still there. She crawled on and let the memories and thoughts fill her. There were fewer here, this room seemed to be private. Quentin's office she realized quickly and she was overwhelmed by the images, the horror and the dark reality.

Dazed and staggering, she hurried out of there, wanting more than ever to help Evelyn. Whatever it took, the vampires had to be stopped. She made it back outside as Chad was unloading the last prostitute.

"Just in time, here comes the chair delivery," Billy said as he pulled the last box out of the back of the truck and Ben closed the door.

Aranha thought about the possibility of making it to wherever Lars might be and back in time to catch that other delivery truck leaving. More importantly, what were the chances Dag wouldn't freak out and do something crazy if she didn't come out with *this* delivery truck?

Worth the risk, she decided and scurried back in the house. She couldn't be certain where he was being kept, but she took the long hallway to a doorway she'd watched Chad drag girls into yesterday. She was able to slip under the doorway by shifting into a smaller spider and she was rewarded with the sight of a dark stairwell heading down. She shifted to something a little bigger for the crawl down. There was enough light coming from a window that she could make out the shape of Lars in a corner, strapped to a chair. He looked alert but he wasn't moving.

She took a minute to make sure they were alone. She didn't hear or see anyone. So she decided to risk revealing herself.

She shifted to human, Lars' eyes locked onto her immediately, wide and disbelieving.

"Shit! If Dag hears I saw you naked, he's going to kill me."

"*That* is what you have to say about this situation?" Aranha laughed, and put her hands on her hips.

"I think it's the biggest threat to my life at the moment," he grumbled.

"Dag has no ownership over my nudity! He needs me to help him with this situation, that's it."

Lars scoffed, "If you really believe that, then you're willfully dumb. Dag has feelings for you, he wants you more than even *he* knows. I could smell it when he came to the house yesterday. Daywalkers, when they meet a webmaker that they are attracted to, not just for sex, mind you, but far deeper, an instinctual bonding kind of attraction; their scent changes. It warns other daywalkers that the woman is theirs. It tells the webmaker that this male has chosen them. If she accepts, she will let him mark her with his scent."

Aranha did a slow blink, waiting for Lars to start laughing and tell her he was making this shit up as he went, but he didn't.

"I don't think that's what's going on, he has said nothing of the sort."

Lars gave a quiet laugh. "That's because he doesn't even know. Most daywalkers that survived the wars never experienced it, or knew anyone who had, the elders were mostly killed off, so no one talked about it. Why reminisce about things that will never happen? Why tease young men with stories of unspeakable love and attraction that they can never possibly have?" Lars' words were serious and held a note of sadness that made her heart ache.

"So how the hell do you know so much?" she whispered with an emotional quake to her voice. The loneliness he was describing hit close to home.

Lars laughed. "I'm a little older than most realize." He winked at her but didn't elaborate.

"They plan to sacrifice you tonight," she said, moving forward to untie his bonds and change the subject. "Don't worry, Dag plans to gather the other daywalkers to storm the place. He was invited to the party, they want witnesses." She shivered.

"I know. You have to leave me."

She looked up from her crouched position, flabbergasted. "They plan to slice your throat open and feed your blood to the girl!"

"I know, and if I'm not here when they come for me, they'll know that their secret is out. I have to stay. I'll be fine, like you said, Dag is gathering a horde to attack." He winked at her and smiled. "My brothers will come for me."

"You might be completely nuts," she whispered.

"Or completely right. Now get out of here before you get caught. I can imagine what would happen if the werewolves found you in here naked."

Aranha frowned up at him. "We'll be here for you tonight,"

she assured him, then loped up the stairs and shifted at the top. If he thought staying was the best tactic, then she would leave him, and she would come back tonight and do everything she could to save him.

She didn't know how much time she had, but she wasn't going to risk missing the chair delivery leaving. She scurried along baseboards, down the hall, through the kitchen and out the door. Ben's delivery truck was gone, as expected, and two more were in its place. Five werewolves and two humans were unloading chairs, tables, and linens.

Aranha crawled onto the bumper of one of the trucks and waited, her mind spinning with information. She wasn't sure how, but they *had* to stop the vampires tonight. Evelyn didn't deserve what they had planned for her.

When the truck made its way through the gate, she jumped and thankfully floated to a spot on the ground this time, rather than halfway up a tree. She crawled as quick as she could into the cover of nearby trees, then shifted and watched for Dag in Lars' truck. She didn't want to stand out in the open and give every passerby a show, so she watched from behind a tree and jumped out when she saw him coming. She didn't wave or holler as she waited. His eyes were searching for her, highly alert, and when they saw her, he swerved off the road and slid to a stop with the passenger door facing her. He leaned over and opened it faster than she could jump to it and he was speeding away before she had it closed.

"What the *fuck* happened in there! Do you have any idea what I was about to do? The truck pulled out twenty minutes ago, where the fuck were you?" His voice was gruff with emotion and fear.

As much as his concern melted her, his aggressive attitude grated her nerves. She yanked her clothes on and hissed at him. "What the fuck do you think I was doing? I saw the opportunity, so I went and found Lars, I had to warn him. I *wanted* to release him."

Dag slammed on the brakes, stopping in the middle of the highway. His knuckles white on the steering wheel. His head turned slowly and she could see the muscles in his jaw bulge as he clenched his teeth. His eyes were the darkest blue she'd ever seen them and his nostrils were flaring. When he spoke, she could see that his fangs were fully extended and there was an extra hiss to his voice.

"You appeared before Lars, naked?" he said carefully.

She had to fight the urge to run, this was the dangerous menace she'd expected to meet all along, this thing that would rather kill her than see her breathe. Except that she was sure it wasn't hatred that was causing him to look at her like that, wasn't *her* he wanted to split in half right now. Lars had warned her; Dag wasn't going to like that she'd had to appear naked in front of him.

"I can't exactly carry around a change of clothes, Dag," she hissed, deciding her best course of action here was going to be annoyance.

Dag hissed, a car honked behind them and swerved around, the man yelled obscenities out the passenger window. Dag didn't even flinch, or look, he was focused on Aranha, eyes boring into hers. "I won't allow him to have you."

"Allow! How dare you presume you have any kind of say in anything I do," Aranha shot back, her hand went to the door handle and she was about to bolt.

He was fast, his arms went around her and suddenly she was on his lap, his fangs were in her neck and her body was on fire. "Fuck!" She screamed as a pleasure beyond anything she'd ever experienced erupted in her body and her own fangs extended. Venom dripping down her chin. Her ass moved against his lap and she could feel his body respond significantly.

She moved her hands up to his head and grasped his braid, holding his lips closer. She made a mewling sound as his fangs retreated, not ready for him to stop, wanting more even if it killed her. As he began to lick at the wounds he'd made, a purring rumble vibrated his chest behind her. She wanted nothing more than to turn around and continue this, take it to its inevitable, pleasurable end.

"Don't test me, Aranha. I'm not sure what I'll do." His voice was low, almost a growl.

"I think I have a pretty good idea." She sniffed and smelled what must be the scent Lars had been talking about. Did Dag really not know? "I think you should let me go and keep driving. I don't want Lars, I don't want anyone... not even you if it means I lose myself, Dag. You can't want to control me and care for me at the same time." She was impressed with her ability to talk so calmly, but she knew it was important; could see that this was a pivotal moment for them. If there was any possibility that they could have some kind of relationship—which she still wasn't convinced she wanted—then he couldn't think to control her every move. She'd been alone for far too long to submit to him just because his fangs could make her melt.

"I want you safe," he hissed.

"Safety is relative," she grumbled and extricated herself from his lap. "And safety is not a trade I'm willing to make for freedom. I think you can understand that." Wasn't that exactly why he lived in the city, away from the daywalker compound? Why he dealt with the vampires regularly? He wanted the freedom to do his own thing. He'd never accept shackles from someone else just to feel safe.

Another car passed, honked and yelled. This time Dag turned and hissed at the passing driver. The man's eyes went wide and his face paled as he stepped on the gas and sped down the road.

Aranha laughed, "He's probably having a heart attack now."

"Maybe he should mind his own goddamn business," Dag grumbled, but started driving.

They stopped when they came across Jonah, running frantically in search of her. He jumped in and hugged her viciously as Dag continued down the road.

"You should stop going in there," Jonah whispered.

"Agreed," she said back with a sigh.

"It smells weird in here," he whispered. "You smell different," he accused.

"Don't worry, everything's fine," she assured Jonah, stroking his hair. She met Dag's eyes briefly, there was a strange, almost fearful look in his eyes.

Dag knew he'd fucked up. Lars had warned him to play it cool, to not overwhelm her or try and push her into anything, but dammit how could he just ignore this overwhelming need that was growing. Knowing that she'd been naked in front of Lars... his hands fisted on the steering wheel as he imagined his friend's eyes sliding over her perfect body, appreciating her curves. He was a man, he would have reacted, if he tried to touch her! Dag stopped himself from thinking in that direction, he didn't want to have to kill his oldest friend, but he would, Aranha was his.

He shot her a sideways glance. She looked deep in thought but her fingers were at her throat, absently touching the spot he'd bitten. There was a small red mark there still, but he knew it would quickly fade. He wasn't even sure why he'd done it. He'd been overwhelmed by anger and jealousy, scared shitless that she was going to leave him. He didn't know what else to do, when he'd grabbed her his only intention had been to keep her in the truck. Her nearness had been too much, his fangs had extended, her head had moved just right and before he knew it, he'd sunk them deep and released an extreme amount of venom he knew would overwhelm her body with pleasurable sensations. A human would have been vibrating with pleasure and need from such a large dose. He'd been surprised and intrigued by her minor reaction.

There hadn't been no reaction of course, her body had heated, she'd let out a small groan as her body moved against his in a delightful way. When he'd pulled back, he could see that her fangs were extended and dripping venom. Her eyes were half closed and her cheeks flushed. She was breathing hard and as she'd spoken, there was a slight tremble to her voice. Her words were forceful, determined, but her voice belied her level of feeling. *Tread carefully.* Lars' words ran through his head again. He had no intention of letting her go, but he would never force her to stay, that wasn't his way. A little voice inside his head was pretty sure he'd tie her to his bed if she tried to run away; he was fairly certain he could resist that little voice if it came down to it.

He just had to figure out how to make sure she understood that he wouldn't harm her, wouldn't desire to have her if it was against her will. He wanted to keep her safe, wanted to keep her for himself, but would never force her. Would never want to watch her wilt in a cage. One thing he was sure she didn't understand; the cage she'd made for herself was more restraining than any he would ever offer.

"You'll want your weapons. We will go to the barn and collect my car."

"Oh! Thanks, yeah I suppose I need a dress for the party as well."

He wanted more than anything to tell her no, you won't be there, it's too dangerous. He didn't, but she was watching him carefully as if expecting it. She was testing him. "Yeah, I suppose you will." It came out a little clenched, but she just nodded and looked out the window so it must have passed.

He let his mind drift to the feeling of her blood pumping through his body. The taste he'd known, but the feeling of it in such a large quantity, it was energizing and fulfilling in a way he'd never experienced, hadn't expected. Was this what it was like to drink from a webmaker, or was this what it was like to drink from someone you cared for? There was so much he felt like he suddenly didn't know, like what the *fuck* was that smell coming off him? Why did he wish she smelled the same... and how was he going to make her his forever?

CHAPTER THIRTEEN

Aranha was still shaken when they got to the barn to retrieve Dag's car and her weapons. She was thankful to get away from him for a moment, space was vital for her sanity.

"Can you drive a stick?" Dag smirked as he handed her the keys to his car.

"I can handle a stick just fine," she said with a wink. The urge to lean in for a kiss was strong, so she did the only thing that she could think, she reached out and smacked his shoulder as if they were old buddies. Then she felt like an idiot as he looked at her a little stunned. "Umm yeah, so where am I getting a dress, and Jonah will need something appropriate I suppose." She said quickly to cover the awkwardness.

"Follow me up the road, there's a mall."

"Sounds like torture," she said with a grin.

"It is, but it'll be the best option I think. Vampires tend to go overboard and if we aren't dressed the part, they might not even let us in."

"And what will you be wearing?" she asked with a raised eyebrow.

"A tux of course." He stepped forward and she stepped back

until she was against the car. He didn't stop until there was a mere breath between their bodies, electricity popped between them and she felt as if he were touching her all over. "You won't be able to take your eyes off me."

"Then how will I know when danger is coming?" she joked, but her voice cracked and he smiled, knowing he was getting to her.

"If I'm there, no danger will get a chance to come at you. Not because I don't think you can handle it, but because I protect what matters."

"And I matter?" she asked, breathless.

"So much." He leaned down and kissed her softly, reached around her and opened the car door. "Now, be nice to my car and follow me."

She stared at him and bit her lip, this was embarrassing. "I don't have any money. I mean I have money, it's just that I don't carry it. I keep it hidden and use it only when I have to because I don't need things usually when I'm out. I don't know if you noticed, but I never did pay you for that beer at the bar and—"

He cut her off with another kiss. "Don't worry, I got you. Just follow me to the horrendous experience that is the mall."

"Fine," she whispered and slumped into the car.

He shut the door and leaned down to the open window. "Aranha."

"Yeah?" she didn't look at him, just busied herself adjusting the seat and starting the car. Jonah was already tucked into the passenger seat, nervously watching their interactions.

"You didn't tell me what you found on the webs in there."

She looked at him then, eyes wide, she couldn't believe they'd gotten so distracted that she hadn't told him. "It's bad, or at least it could be if it works. They plan to sacrifice Lars and they are trying to resurrect Eve."

"As in..."

"Yeah, Eve as in Mother of All. I can't be certain, but it has something to do with breeding."

"Vampires can't breed," Dag said with a scoff.

"I know, so why do they want to resurrect—or reincarnate I'm not sure what they really think they're doing—Eve into the girl, Evelyn."

"They must think they can gain the ability through Eve, she's the original mother, the original breeder."

"If they can so easily create more vampires!"

"Yeah, that would be disastrous for everyone. They'd wipe out the human population in a thousand years, but what does Lars have to do with it?"

"Something about his blood, I couldn't tell for sure."

"We'll stop them. Sten won't be able to stand by and let this happen, he'll have to send everyone in." He looked over at Jonah, sitting happily in the passenger seat. "Don't let her grind the gears too much, I love this car."

"Yes, sir. This car is beautiful," Jonah agreed quickly.

He nodded and walked to the truck. Their mission was more important than whatever else was going on between them. Whatever it took, they had to stop the vampires.

"Sir?" she asked Jonah as they followed Dag out onto the road.

"You like him?" Jonah asked shyly.

"I don't know."

Jonah looked thoughtful. "He likes you, and I think he will protect you. So you should stay close to him and I will never like him more than I love you, but I will be loyal to anyone you are with. I will still rip his fucking throat out if he hurts you," he said seriously.

She wasn't sure how to respond to that, so she just patted his leg and followed Dag to a crowded mall. She kept her sunglasses on to keep the humans from seeing her disturbing eyes. Of course it might not have mattered, most were so busy staring at Dag they barely noticed her. Dag was tall, blond and beautiful. He was also wearing a frown that bordered on murderous.

"Having fun?" she asked as a mother grabbed her children and rushed into a nearby store when she saw them coming.

"What are you talking about?"

"You're scaring the shit out of everyone. Maybe don't look like you want to murder someone."

Dag laughed and his face broke into a smile that was just as distracting as his frown. "My mind is on our coming battle, so yeah, accurate assessment of my face I guess."

"Well relax, or we are going to get questioned by the mall cops. I think they are already following us. They probably think you've kidnapped Jonah and I."

"Why would they think that?"

"Because you're gripping my arm like you're using it to drag me around and I'm wearing dark glasses, probably hiding a black eye because you abuse me. Jonah just always looks... lost."

Dag gasped, "I would never hit a woman!"

"Yeah, well you look like you're on steroids so maybe chill, let my arm go and smile slightly."

"It would help if Jonah didn't look like he's just been kidnapped, maybe they're following him," Dag hissed.

Aranha looked over at Jonah, he was walking hunched, close to her side and slightly behind. She grabbed his hand and pulled him forward. "Stand tall, you're safe."

"Yeah, until he freaks out and turns wolf," Dag hissed. "Is it even safe for him to be in public?" He moved his hand to her back, still touching and guiding, but not pulling. His face relaxed into an easy smile and now the looks they were getting from passing humans were more appreciative and less frightened, so that was good.

"We've practiced shopping, he's fine he just doesn't trust

people. He's been hurt." She tried to convey with her eyes how intensely Jonah had been hurt. She wasn't sure Dag fully comprehended, but he did reach around Aranha and touch the boy lightly on the shoulder.

"Don't worry, Jonah, I've got you."

Jonah made a sound that might have been close to a purr and his face brightened. Dag's acceptance seemed to relieve something deep inside of him and tugged on something deep inside of Aranha as well.

Dag tried to take them into a shop with a wedding dress in the window. She immediately dug in her heels. "No way, there won't be anything in there I want to wear."

"What do you mean?"

"I may have to dress up, but I still get to be me and unless they've got a selection of black and tight, I don't think it'll work."

Dag laughed, "Alright let's keep looking."

They came to a store with a goth mannequin wearing a plaid skirt and Aranha hurried in, this was definitely her style. She went up to the girl behind the counter, she had purple hair and a nose ring, this was her kind of human. "I need a cocktail dress. Do you have anything like that?"

The girl looked Aranha up and down, not convinced she was in the right store. Her eyes went to Jonah and she gave him a wide smile. "We have a few prom dresses in the back, leftover from the spring. Are you looking for anything?" she asked Jonah. "I like that hair color." She touched her own. "I thought about doing that, but went with this instead because it's kind of been my signature for a while."

"Oh, yeah, blue," Jonah said quietly.

The girl frowned, obviously disappointed in Jonah's lack of interest. She walked toward the back of the store.

Aranha gave Jonah a confused look. Dag poked him with his

elbow and Jonah gave him a hurt look. Dag huffed, frustrated. "She's into you," he whispered.

"What?" Jonah asked, genuinely confused.

"The girl was complimenting you. You respond with a compliment and a question," Dag said.

"Oh... okay!" Jonah finally caught on. They all followed the girl to the back of the store. "I like purple." Jonah said awkwardly.

The girl gave him a bright smile. "Thanks, I might keep it like this for a while, like I said, it's been my signature color for a while now."

"These dresses look great, I'll try some on. Jonah you should pick something out too, something dressy. What do you have here for him?" Aranha asked the girl.

The girl's eyes brightened. "This way, I have some really cool stuff." She grabbed Jonah's hand and pulled him to the other side of the store, leaving Aranha and Dag alone.

"She's going to eat him alive," Dag said.

"If he doesn't eat her first," she laughed. "Now, which dresses should I try?"

By the time they left, Aranha had picked a dress with jewelry to match, Jonah had a whole outfit and the girl's phone number. Dag had paid for it all without comment. He even slipped Jonah some cash and told him to ask the girl to get a smoothie, since she was hinting so strongly that it was time for her break.

Aranha couldn't help smiling as her and Dag walked back through the mall.

"What?" he finally asked as they hit the parking lot.

"Is this like, a date?"

Dag laughed, "Sweetie, if this were a date, you'd already be naked."

She stopped walking and waited for him to realize it and

turn. When he did, she saw a wicked smile on his face that told her he was *not* joking.

"Babe," she said slowly, then started walking, swinging her ass in a way she knew he'd like. "If I ever *let* you take me on a date, you'd be ending the night in chains."

She heard him hiss as she passed and she knew she'd hit it right.

He caught her in two strides, pulled her back against him and grabbed her chin, forcing her head to turn. "Don't threaten me with a good time," he whispered then flicked his tongue out and caressed her lips.

"Don't manhandle me," she whispered back.

He let go immediately, but he didn't move away and neither did she. "No desire to force you, remember."

"So you say." She moved slightly and let their lips touch. She led the kiss, pressing and coaxing him to respond. When he did, she nearly lost her balance. His arms slid around her easily, keeping her upright as he deepened the kiss. Her body melded to his.

"Get a room!" someone shouted, followed by a honk and a car racing around them.

Dag pulled away and smiled at her. "We are always getting yelled at when we kiss, what do you think that means?"

"I think it means you pick the worst possible moments to be irresistibly aggressive."

Dag laughed and put an arm around her back, guiding her to where they'd parked. When they got there, she moved quickly to separate from him. His closeness was dangerously distracting.

"So, what's my dad like?" she asked, to effectively kill any romantic feelings hanging around.

"Basic asshole in charge for far too long with ideas of grandeur."

"Cool, so that's where I get it from," she winked.

"You're destined to be queen, that's pretty grand."

"Ah, but are you destined to be my king?"

"You better hope he thinks so, otherwise he might decide to sell you to the highest bidder. Worse yet, loan you out for reproductive purposes." Dag's expression darkened and his hands fisted. She could tell he thought these were all likely scenarios and there was only one that she thought she could live with, even temporarily.

Aranha took a deep breath, she had to do something she might regret later. "I need you to mark me with your scent."

"What?"

"Lars said that when a daywalker meets someone they want to be with, they start producing a scent that marks them as taken, and they mark the webmaker with it as well, to warn off others. I think I've smelled it on you. You need to mark me so that Sten and everyone else is sure to know."

Dag grinned wide, his fangs running out. "Well step into my room." He swung the back door of the truck open and held out a hand.

"I don't think it involves sex," Aranha said with a huff.

Dag crossed his arms over his chest. "Yeah? What do you think it involves?"

"I don't know, Lars didn't say, isn't it just like, instinctual? What do you feel like rubbing on me?"

"*Babe...*" Dag drawled in a way that put a very specific picture in her mind and her face flamed.

"Okay, stupid question."

"Not stupid. Very intriguing actually." He grabbed her waistband and pulled her forward. "If I don't know, you'll just have to sniff it out, darling. Where do *you* want to rub yourself?"

"Not having sex with you," she said again, just to be sure. "Not in a goddamn parking lot, not in the back of Lars' truck and *not* because you have to mark me to keep my father from selling me to someone else."

"I would take you in a parking lot, in anyone's backseat and for any reason." He pulled her to him roughly and nipped at her neck lightly. "I will wait for you to specify that it's time, though," he whispered in her ear. "I'm not an animal."

She trembled and tried to keep her resolve to not experience him in such a public and high school fashion. "Well then, sit back and let me sniff."

He spread his arms wide and stood still for her. Aranha took her time, starting at his face. She trailed her nose across his forehead, cheeks, lips even. Definitely not from his fangs, that would have been too easy. She moved around his neck, nothing.

She couldn't resist biting his earlobe though. "Guess I have to go lower, hold on, cowboy."

He trembled slightly but didn't give up his position. She sniffed each arm and hand, laying a kiss in each palm before moving on, back to his throat.

She stopped a moment and looked into his eyes. "Lower?" she asked with a saucy half smile.

"I would never turn that down," he said with a wink.

"Please remove your shirt," she instructed.

He quickly obliged then spread his arms again.

She trailed along his collarbone and then lower. She knew before she got there, could smell it getting stronger. "Here," she said, surprised. She laid a hand over his heart, feeling it race beneath her palm.

He lowered his arms. "Well, it could have been more fun than that! I guess, rub away," he laughed.

She rubbed her cheeks, shoulders and arms over the spot, feeling like a cat in heat by the time she was done.

"I hope this works."

"It would be better if you took off your shirt," he said with a mockingly serious tone.

"Ha, and risk you taking advantage?" She winked at him and stepped away.

"What did I miss?" Jonah asked carefully as he joined them.

"Just preparing for the next big adventure," Aranha said, taking a deep breath. "How was the smoothie?"

"Great, Tara is nice," he said quietly and his cheeks turned a bright red.

"Yeah, I think so too," Aranha gave him a little squeeze.

"Are you ready for this?" Dag asked. "It's just a short drive from here."

"I guess I have to be."

"Just follow me, and don't worry, scent or no, I won't let anything happen to you. Either of you."

"I have your shield, right?" she said with a half smile.

"Right," he said with a deep seriousness.

"Thank you," she said quietly and walked to the car. No use putting this off.

"Are you sure we can trust him?" Jonah asked as he got in the passenger seat.

"Yeah, I am." And she was, she knew he wouldn't let anything happen to them, she just wasn't sure she wanted the consequences of his devotion.

"You smell," Jonah whispered.

"Yeah, it's his mark, apparently it'll keep the other daywalkers away from me."

Jonah just wrinkled his nose and rolled down the window. "I don't like it, it doesn't smell like you."

Aranha smiled as she drove, she kind of liked the scent.

As Dag pulled out of the mall parking lot, with Aranha and Jonah in his car behind him, he was wound so tight he thought he might explode. It took every ounce of self-control to be so close to her, so intimate with her and not push her back into the truck and take her.

He smiled as he replayed the way she'd touched him, the way she'd teased. How she'd sniffed her way down to the spot where his claiming scent was coming from. He'd known where it was, he just hadn't known *what* it was until she'd told him what Lars had said.

If he never had her in any other way, that memory of touch would get him through a hundred years of lonely nights.

She was his, no denying it, and he was leading her into a pack of daywalkers ready to tear her apart in their urgency to have her first. If she survived that, he was going to take her into the middle of a bunch of bloodthirsty psychopaths who would kill her as soon as they knew what she was.

"Fuck!" he yelled and hit the steering wheel. What was he doing? What choices did he have?

He took a calming breath. He was doing what he had to in order to save her and the human population. His choices were no good all the way around and at least this one... this one was a warrior's way.

He looked into the rearview mirror and saw her behind the wheel of his car singing and shaking her head. *She* was a warrior too, otherwise she would have run from the start, she never would have bothered trying to find out what the vampires were up to, or how to possibly save one innocent human girl.

He turned off the main road and started down the long drive that would lead to the daywalker compound. He was ready to fight his brothers for the warrior he'd claimed as his own. He hoped he wouldn't have to.

The number of cars outside told him that Jeb had succeeded

in alerting all the others. Everyone was home and as he pulled to a stop, they all came out onto the porch. These were his brothers, but he would kill any who touched Aranha.

Sten pushed to the front of the group, arms crossed and glaring. The deceit of yesterday was probably about to bite him in the ass today.

Dag got out and walked around the truck, his plan was to open her door, take her hand and present her to his clan properly.

He should have known she wasn't going to go for that.

She was out of the car, a knife in both hands and she was stalking toward the porch. Jonah was close behind her, slinking along cautiously.

"Alright assholes, which one of you thinks you have the right to call yourself my father and thinks you have any chance in hell of telling me who or what I am going to be doing?"

Dag smiled and pride filled him. His chest puffed and he crossed his arms over his chest, looking from her to Sten. This was his warrior woman, she didn't need him, but he was here anyway.

CHAPTER FOURTEEN

Aranha had made a couple decisions on the drive. She'd blasted eighties rock and screamed out her frustrations, allowing her mind to settle. She knew she wanted Dag; knew she could accept a life, at least for a time, with him. She knew she had no intention of walking into a situation that was out of her control with her newly discovered dad and his horde of followers. She refused to be anyone's brood mare, and she had to keep Jonah safe. She was sure of all of these things and she needed a plan to go along with them.

The first step, establish dominance. So she got out of the car before Dag could open her door. She was holding two of her favorite knives and she strode forward with an aggressive stance. She looked at the group of disturbingly similar looking men and began on her own terms. No one would look at her and think she was malleable. She was no frightened deer and her life was her own.

She stated her position, her voice steady and filled with conviction. Her eyes flicked from face to face, judging reactions. They varied from surprise to amusement.

A man who looked no older than the rest, stepped

forward. Long blond hair braided back at the sides of his head, green eyes and an easy smile. "That would be me. My daughter, you have finally come home." He spread his arms wide as if he expected her to run forward and accept an embrace.

"No thanks, I have one. I also have a boyfriend, so you can just stop thinking you'll be selling breeding rights off to your buddies here."

"You can't mean that frightened wolf?" His voice was shocked and his eyes wide. No doubt he was thinking about how webmakers behaved in mating situations, survival for a werewolf was rare.

Dag stepped forward. "Not the wolf," he said, putting a hand on her shoulder but remaining slightly behind.

She couldn't have appreciated his actions more. He was letting her lead this, letting her show her strength, only offering support. "I've claimed Dag, I bear his scent and will take no others."

She wanted to eye the crowd, see what kind of reaction the men would have to this news, but she didn't dare take her gaze off Sten. Sten's eyes widened slightly, the only indication of shock.

"I never thought Dag would be one to settle down, you'll have to forgive my shock. He didn't indicate a care for you when we spoke yesterday and I didn't take him for having aspirations to be king. Did he tell you that you and your chosen mate are to be crowned?" His smile was sly.

She felt Dag stiffen behind her, she reached up and laid a hand on his, still clutching her blade. "I know about your promises. Unfortunately neither Dag, nor I, have any care for such foolishness."

"And the wolf? Why is he cowering behind you?"

"This is Jonah, my son." She stated proudly. She didn't need to explain anything more to this man, he hadn't earned a right to know her life, or Jonah's.

"I see, well then, welcome Jonah."

Jonah stepped forward slightly and grasped Aranha's arm.

Sten's eyes narrowed slightly. "We have much to discuss, please come in. I am sure you're curious about where you come from and I believe you two have some information about the vampires to relay."

"We do." She stepped forward and Dag was right beside her, hand on her back. Aranha put away her blades, knowing they were still easily accessible. She wanted to show that she had no intention of harming anyone who didn't intend to harm her, but she was willing to kill any who did.

Sten turned and shooed the others. Aranha took the opportunity to study them a bit. None of them looked angry about the situation. Some eyed her lustfully, some shot jealous looks at Dag, but none were aggressive, none made her feel as if they were going to try and take her for themselves. She relaxed slightly.

"Brothers," Dag said quietly as they passed through the parted throng.

"Not sure if I should be jealous, or thankful that I'm not saddled with one woman for the rest of my life," one man said, stepping forward to pat Dag on the shoulder. "I'm Calder." He held out a hand to Aranha.

"Aranha," she said and shook his hand.

"I hear you spent some time with Lars."

"Yeah, great guy. He's a little tied up at the moment, but wouldn't let me save him for fear of giving away our position."

Calder laughed. "That sounds like Lars. He's a good man."

After that she shook about twenty other hands and was given names she would never remember. With each one, she felt

Dag relax beside her. These were his brothers and they were accepting the situation.

When they finally made it to where Sten was waiting in his library, Aranha was feeling mostly relaxed as well. She felt secure in the relationship she was portraying, and safe among Dag's clan brothers. Unfortunately she wasn't sure how she felt about her father and didn't know what his intentions really were. She was still on alert.

Sten was seated on a throne-like chair, looking like he was expecting to be praised accordingly. Aranha was shocked to see Dag walk over and bend to kiss his hand. She was *not* about to do that crap. She took a seat across from Sten, pulling Jonah to sit at her feet, and waited. She met Sten's eyes over Dag's back and lifted an eyebrow.

"Join your fiancée," Sten said, pulling his hand away and watching Aranha.

Dag stood and when he turned from Sten, his face showed what he really thought of this ceremony. It was all part of the game, Aranha understood. It allowed Dag to continue to live unbothered and alone, she wouldn't think less of him for it, but it did make her like Sten a little less. Dag sat beside her on the couch and laid a familiar hand on her knee.

"You look like your mother," Sten said with a wistful smile.

"What can you tell me of your experience with my mother before I was born?" Aranha asked. Her mother hadn't ever talked about the courtship and relationship with Sten. She'd always assumed it was just too painful for her to speak of, so she'd never asked.

"Oh, Carinen was a lovely creature. We met in France when there were hardly any webmakers left. I don't think she had anyone left of her clan. She was alone and scared. I offered her my shield the moment I found her hiding in a dark forest. We immediately connected, but she was hunted, we both were.

We had to continuously move or be at risk. When she became pregnant, her fears were compounded. We found peace for a short time in Portugal, but as you know, she left there when you were but an infant, too afraid of what would happen to you. I think she wouldn't have worried so much if you were male. I had been running for a long time as well, my clan was killed off by the vampires in France. It was such a wretched time for all of us. I was sure," he paused for a moment, taking a deep breath and it was the first real sign of emotion he showed. "I was sure that you and she had both perished soon after. Please, tell me of your childhood, were you happy?"

"Well, we moved around a lot, as you can imagine. She loved me and she tried her best to keep me safe. I didn't know that any daywalkers existed anymore, until I met Dag, and I thought they were as bloodthirsty as the vampires. So that was a surprise."

"How did your mother die?"

"Vampire," Aranha said without elaboration.

"And other webmakers? Have you run across more of your kind? Did Carinen mention any others?" There was excitement and hope in his voice.

"No, she thought we were alone. I've never come across any others in all these years. I could very well be the last."

"How is it that you have managed to survive so long alone?" He was skeptical.

"I move a lot; I kill only those who deserve it so I don't draw attention to myself; my mother taught me that before she died. I keep nothing I don't need and I stick to the shadows. In my experience, most werewolves and vampires don't expect me to exist and they don't recognize my scent when they come across it. So I have not had any issues, until I walked into Dag's bar on accident."

"Ah yes, and you went home with him that night, but didn't

stay long I hear, and he didn't even know what you were." Sten's tone and expression showed clearly that he didn't believe any bit of that, but wasn't going to outright call Dag a liar. "Yet now you two are in love?"

"I appreciate that you sent all your men to find me and make sure that I was safe," she said with as much sarcasm as she could muster. If he didn't mention Dag's lie, she would keep the fact that he wanted to breed her out to his men out of the conversation as well. "Dag and I are committed to each other, yes."

"Of course! I care deeply, you are my child. As soon as I heard your description, I knew it must be you. In all these years I have heard of no other webmaker. Not from my clan, not from any other immortal."

"It's too bad you couldn't have reproduced more with my mother, huh."

He had the decency to look offended by her implication. "I loved your mother deeply! Our relationship had nothing to do with reproduction of the species. I never would have left her side. It isn't the way of daywalkers, to leave the one they mark. I was bound to her for all of eternity and beyond. As Dag is to you now."

Aranha briefly choked on air at this statement. Dag made no move beside her, as if he knew all about this. What the hell had she agreed to? She recovered quickly and focused on the more important question. "So you would agree to us not having children?"

"I accept that it is beyond my control," he said between clenched teeth. "Of course I would implore you to think of the implications of our two species going extinct at some point. Would the earth remain in balance?"

"Consideration is all I will promise," she said.

Dag remained stiff and silent beside her. In a way, this

conversation had nothing to do with him, she was the only female, if she said no, there would be no children.

"Now, tell me of the vampires' plans."

Dag stepped in here, telling Sten what they had found out and their plan to not only save Lars, but to stop the ceremony and save Evelyn, as well.

When Dag finished, Sten sat back and looked thoughtful. "The vampires are trying to resurrect Eve. That is something I never thought I would come across. We have regained the power of repopulation in Aranha, or at least the possibility. They will see this as a great threat to their own cause. She must not go."

"Fuck that! I can fight and I will *not* sit back while that innocent girl is possibly harmed. Besides, I don't think they will recognize me easily. I've managed to hide so long they don't think I exist."

Sten narrowed his eyes and his nostrils flared, he was not used to being argued with. "Your fiery attitude matches your mother's. I should expect nothing less of our child." There was a slight sense of pride in his words.

"Thanks," she said, assuming it was a backhanded compliment.

"But you must see what I mean. Your presence could seriously inhibit our operation," Sten added calmly.

Aranha hated it, but she knew he was right to worry. If they recognized what she was, it would be a problem. "I could sneak in easy enough, appear at the right time. Or stay back with a group of daywalkers? Do you all intend to waltz into the party uninvited?"

"That is exactly what I intend, actually. We will go in as a group, they can fight us at the gate or let us in, I bet they'll let us in. They are over confident fools." He looked thoughtful. "You went in and out twice, the werewolves didn't notice?"

"They didn't seem to. The one at the gate, he seemed to notice something different, he watched the delivery truck go by, but it wasn't enough to set off an alarm. I don't think he knew *what* he was smelling."

"That's good, and they didn't find and destroy your webs?"

"No, one was gone when I went back, but I would count that as accidental. The other two were perfectly intact."

Sten nodded thoughtfully. "I think your scent will be well hidden among us. We can present you as a mere human companion if you keep your eyes down and don't shake any hands. The boy will blend fine, he can go in as our pet as well."

"I think we can handle that." Aranha looked to Dag, he didn't look happy about the plan but wasn't arguing either. "I believe Dag will keep us safe."

"I will," he said firmly.

"You won't order her to stay behind?" Sten asked with a sly smile.

"I won't order her to do anything, she is my partner and mine to protect, I don't own her." Dag lifted his chin and dared Sten to tell him this was the wrong way to do things.

"Dag, why don't you and Jonah go talk to the others. Let them know what the plan is. I would love a few moments with my daughter."

Aranha met Dag's gaze and gave a slight nod. She wasn't afraid to be alone with Sten, she didn't fully trust him, but she wasn't afraid of him either. She gave Jonah a reassuring smile and he rose slowly.

Dag didn't want to leave them alone, but new he had no excuse not to and if Aranha was okay with it, he would be too. He kissed her lips briefly, making sure to continue the guise of a relationship, but also because he craved her touch like air in his lungs.

Jonah whined but followed Dag out when Aranha gave him a reassuring smile. "Don't worry, she's far too important for Sten to harm."

Jonah didn't look convinced.

They went in search of his clan brothers. They were easy to find, gathered in the back of the house picking out weapons and discussing strategies. Jonah slunk behind him, practically shivering with fear. Dag wasn't sure how to fix that, without Aranha there, Jonah had no confidence.

"Brothers," he called to gather their attention. He put a hand on Jonah's shoulder, hoping his touch would calm the boy.

"Tell us you are in this for pleasure, brother. If not, I think any one of us would gladly take that beauty off your hands," Calder called out with a laugh.

Dag smiled. "She is mine till death, boys. Find your own."

They all laughed at that, but a sadness settled over them as well, because the reality was, none existed.

Dag relayed the information pertinent to the night's activities and instructed them on the vague plan. "Most importantly, we can't let them notice what Aranha is, not until it's too late. They will see her as quite a threat, but she is too valuable to gather information and fight to leave behind. She'll need to be covered at all times to keep them from scenting her."

"She'll be a top priority, we all know how important she is," Calder assured him.

Dag could see the wheels turning in the minds around him. If Aranha was alive, could others be out there too? If Dag and Aranha were able to reproduce females... Dag didn't like that line of thought at all and started to wonder if Aranha's implication that they might be better off not reproducing, was the right way to go. Could he ever imagine handing off one of his daughters to one of these men? And what of sons? They would be destined to be alone forever. No, it was better to let the lines end with them, but they were going to take the vampires and werewolves with them if at all possible.

"Get your minds out of the gutter boys, we have a fight to prepare for!" Dag yelled and they all whooped in response.

"And what of the boy?" Calder asked quietly as the others started to talk of the coming fight. "He's not really her son?"

Jonah tried to shrink behind Dag as Calder spoke. Dag pulled him forward and gave him a smile. "Jonah is important to Aranha. She saved him, adopted him as her own and he's devoted to her. So, he is important to me," Dag made sure he met Calder's eyes and conveyed the message. Jonah was to be treated like one of them.

"A handsome new brother then," Calder said loudly. "Jonah, I look forward to getting to know you better."

"Oh... okay," Jonah said quietly, his voice shaking.

Dag wasn't sure what had the boy so nervous, but it concerned him deeply. If Jonah was going to be a part of this family, he'd have to stop presenting himself as a frightened victim. He gave the boy a light pat on the back. "Let me show you to your room."

As they left the others, Jonah was hanging onto Dag's arm like he often did to Aranha. Dag was confused and disappointed that what should have been a reassuring interaction had somehow backfired so badly.

Dag got their bags and took them to a row of rooms behind the main house that had once served as servant's quarters. They weren't much, but they had a bed and bathroom. They served their purpose. He took Jonah to one he knew was unused. "You can stay in this one. Relax and we'll come for you when it's time to go."

Jonah looked worried and shaky, biting his lip and crossing his arms over his chest.

Dag sighed heavily. "You are going to have to relax man. Aranha is fine."

"Oh... yeah I know she's fine, she's so strong." His face was sullen and he was picking at his nails nervously.

"And you are fine," he added.

"Yeah, I—I don't want to get to know your brothers," he said quietly.

Dag was shocked, "Why?"

"I mean." Tears started to run down Jonah's face. "I'm sorry, sir, I just."

Realization dawned on Dag and anger filled him at the unfairness of this boy's life. Bitten by a monster and then abused by more. No one deserved that. He sighed heavily. "No one here is going to harm you. Whatever happened to you before, it won't ever happen again. This is a safe place."

"Okay," Jonah whispered.

Dag wasn't sure what to do to help the boy, to make him believe, but he pulled him in for a quick hug. "Aranha would kill anyone who even thought of harming you."

"She's not here," he whispered.

"No, but I am, and I would kill anyone who tried to harm you." He looked down into the fear filled eyes of the boy and saw him relax just slightly. "Those are my brothers. They are your brothers now, too and we protect each other. You and Aranha belong to our clan now. Chosen family is often stronger than the ones we are born into."

"Okay," he whispered, looking better. "She saved me," he said quietly. "I know I'm a burden, I try to be helpful, but... I will try to be helpful here too."

"You are just fine, Jonah. It takes time to get over something as horrible as I can only imagine you went through. She was sent by the gods to be your savior, and she is doing a great job as far as I can tell. Now she's got our help, though."

Jonah gave him a half smile. "You love her?"

"Something like that," Dag said, a little uncomfortable.

"She needs saving too," he whispered and went into the room. "Oh cool, TV."

Dag rolled his eyes, shut the door and moved down to his own room, he hadn't been there in a long time, but it was kept for him in case he ever needed it. Aranha wasn't there yet and to distract himself from the strong desire to go find her, he showered.

CHAPTER FIFTEEN

"Just promise me you'll think about what I said," Sten said as he showed Aranha to Dag's room.

"I will," she assured him. She hurried into the small apartment-like room and away from Sten. It was just missing a kitchenette and it would be exactly like many of the places she'd lived in over the years. Room for a bed, a chair, a television and a dresser. There was a door leading to a bathroom, she could hear the shower running. Her bags were on the dresser and Dag's boots were on the floor by the bed.

Aranha dropped onto the bed with a sigh and thought over the conversation she'd had with Sten. He wanted her to not only reconsider her bond with Dag, but to accept being crowned queen. Queen of what exactly, she wasn't sure, and he hadn't been too specific. They weren't exactly a huge thriving group, and he knew it.

The bathroom door opened and she was sufficiently dragged from her brooding. Dag stood in the doorway with a towel wrapped around his waist, water dripping down his bare chest. His hair was loose and wet, hanging long around him. Her mouth went dry, her eyes taking in every delicious inch of him. Her tongue flicked out as her eyes trailed a rivulet flow from his neck, around a dark nipple, and into his belly button.

"Fuck," she whispered.

His answer was a low growl as he dropped his towel. Her eyes shot up to his face, locking eyes with him. Was she ready for this? Could she handle this? Did she care?

"You tell me no now and I'll walk back in that bathroom and take care of myself," he said in a low gravelly voice that made her body heat instantly. Suddenly all of her clothing felt too tight and she wasn't sure if she was breathing.

"Yes," she managed to strangle out of her closing throat.

He grinned and walked forward, never breaking eye contact. She popped up on her elbows as he approached, ready for everything he had to offer. She couldn't hold back a giggle.

He stopped and raised an eyebrow. "Something funny?"

"No, I—I was just thinking about how I don't have to worry about killing you."

He laughed and leaned down to kiss her lips. "As long as you keep those knives out of it, we should be okay." He let his fangs extend and scraped them lightly over her lips. "Take off your clothes," he ordered and she shivered as she hurried to comply.

There was no big reveal here, he'd already seen her naked a couple times in the last few days. She was soon kneeling on the bed before him, naked and eager, fangs out and dripping venom. "You promise I won't hurt you?" she asked.

"I encourage you to try."

He pulled her to him and the feeling of flesh against flesh was enough to make her groan. He was so warm! His body was hard in all the right places, and he smelled so damn good! She wrapped her arms around his back and let her nails dig in as his lips caressed her neck. Her lower body bucked forward, caressing him. He grabbed her ass and pulled her tighter against him as his fangs sank deep into her neck. He sucked lightly and licked at the wounds, then captured her mouth in a metallic kiss. The taste of her own blood on his tongue was unexpectedly erotic.

"Dag, I need you," she whispered against his mouth.

"I can feel that, unfortunately you're just going to have to wait for it," he said with a grin, then he slid down her body, trailing wet kisses as he went. When he got where he was going, she had her hands in his hair and she was gasping for air. If he hadn't had his hands on her hips, holding her up, she never would have been able to stay upright.

When he laid her back and leaned over her with a look of pure satisfaction on his face, she was ready to throw him down and take what she needed. He moved quickly, shoving her legs apart and filling her. She pulled his head down and as their bodies moved in a quick steady rhythm, she sank her fangs into his flesh and lapped at the release of his blood into her waiting mouth.

"Fuck, yes," he groaned, holding her head to his neck, encouraging her to drink deep.

Her body responded to his encouragement, four spider arms extended from her sides and wrapped around him as she exploded in a release so intense, she wasn't sure it would ever stop. Her body convulsed, her eyes closed, and she let the feeling ride her until she was left shivering and breathing in gasps.

When it stopped, she was afraid to open her eyes, afraid to see terror or disgust on his face; or a dead body on top of her, that had happened before. She lay there, perfectly still and slowing her breathing.

"Aranha, love? Are you alright?" he whispered, pushing a lock of hair off her face.

She opened her eyes and saw only concern on his face. He

leaned down and kissed her gently. When he pulled up, his mouth was covered in blood, his blood this time. Her hands ran down his back, it was sticky with blood as well, from where her spider legs had dug into his flesh.

"Did I hurt you?" she asked quietly.

He laughed, long and loud. He flopped onto his back and pulled her to his side.

"I'm glad you find my concern amusing," she grumbled as she cuddled close and laid her head on his shoulder. His arm was around her and she couldn't imagine a better place to be.

"I told you, you can't kill me that easy. I'm no frail human, a little flesh wound isn't going to bother me." He laughed again. "And now I understand the four round scars I see on the backs of so many of the older guys."

Aranha bit her lip, she really didn't want to talk about that part, it had happened before and she had hoped maybe he hadn't noticed. She buried her face in his shoulder and groaned. "Sorry about that."

"Don't be sorry! I will wear them like a badge of honor." He forced her to meet his gaze and he wasn't laughing now. "I don't think you understand, I am in this; you are mine and I am yours and there will be no going back."

"What if I don't want children?"

"Then we don't have children."

"What if I don't want to be queen?"

"What about me makes you think I have any interest in being king?" He raised one eyebrow sardonically.

She smiled at him shyly. "Okay, we can try this thing."

He kissed her nose. "As if I was going to give you any other option," he said with a wink.

"I got blood in your clean hair." She lifted a lock for inspection.

"Hmm, I guess I'll have to let you wash it." He moved quickly, picking her up and carrying her to the shower.

She caught sight of the bed behind them, covered in blood. They were going to ruin a lot of sheets.

It took a while, but they finally emerged from the bathroom, clean and satisfied. He tossed her a shirt he pulled out of a drawer. "I keep things here still, just in case."

Aranha slipped on the large t-shirt, his smell surrounded her and she couldn't help smiling. Was this what it was like to have a boyfriend? Easy and fun?

"Will you braid my hair?" he asked.

"Of course! Take a seat." She settled onto the edge of the bed and he sat on the floor. She brushed out his long locks then French braided them in one thick long braid down the center of his head and down his back. It was a surprisingly intimate experience. When she was done, he looked up appreciatively and she leaned down and kissed him.

"Your turn?"

"Oh! Sure, that would be great."

They switched spots and he braided her hair in two French braids on the sides of her head, leaving the middle long and smoothed back. The effect was fierce and elegant, perfect for a party that was going to end in a battle.

"Wow, you're pretty good at that."

"Years of practice."

She sighed heavily. "I wish this didn't have to end."

"What's that?"

"This little cocoon. It feels like nothing else exists but us in this moment. I wish we could just stay in here forever."

"We could, theoretically. I can feed off you. How long can you live on blood alone?"

"I don't know, but it doesn't matter because we have a party to attend and a human to save."

"A resurrection to stop."

"And your brother to rescue."

"Well, I suppose we can test your blood tolerance some other time," he laughed. "It would be an interesting experiment."

They dressed for the party. Her dress was a floor length, tight, black, cocktail dress with a slit up to her thigh on both sides. It came with a wide, black and red leather corset belt that tied in the back and provided a perfect spot for some of her smallest blades. The neckline was plunging and the sleeves short and off the shoulders. She'd picked out a red choker with a spider on it and earrings to match. Her shoes were red patent leather and as she stood in front of the mirror, she felt beautiful and she felt like a warrior ready to battle for the innocent.

Dag walked up behind her, looking like a model in a black suit and tie. "Beautiful," he said and leaned down to kiss her bare shoulder. "Maybe too beautiful, the plan was to have you blend, perhaps we should have picked out a suit?"

"Too late for that, I guess I'll just have to trust you to keep me safe while I save the day."

"I've got your back, forever." His eyes met hers in the mirror and the promise she saw there melted her heart.

"And I've got yours, don't underestimate me."

"I wouldn't dare," he promised.

It was something new and amazing, to be valued for what she was, to be truly seen and appreciated. She'd spent her life hiding, doing good from the shadows, no one knowing how many she'd saved, how often she'd dealt out punishment for evil. This man saw her, understood her powers, her instincts, and her needs. He knew what she was capable of and he still wanted her. It was overwhelming.

A quiet knock on the door caught their attention. "Come in," Dag called.

Jonah walked in wearing black slacks and a black button up. His eyes shot to the blood covered bed and he looked horrified. His eyes whipped to Aranha with a questioning look. She gave him a smile. "You look great," she said, trying to ease the awkward moment.

"Let me do your hair," Dag said quickly. "A warrior doesn't let it get in his way."

"Oh, okay," Jonah said quietly and walked over to sit where Dag had indicated. "You look nice, Aranha," he said as Dag began to quickly French braid.

"Thank you," she said, striking a quick pose and laughing.

"You should consider shaving up the sides," Dag said.

"Aranha keeps trying to cut it."

"No, just the sides, leave the top long," Dag instructed.

"Yes, sir."

"Dag," Dag corrected and patted him on the back. "Looks good, ready?"

"Let's go kick some ass," Aranha said, emotion deepening her voice. This was her little family of sorts, and she just might like that more than she ever thought possible.

Dag wanted to say so much, but he knew it wasn't the time. The experience of being with her, of seeing her let go and really be herself was amazing. Her energy was all consuming and it was so bright and warm, he hadn't expected that. He could imagine a life with her, could imagine them in his condo, running the bar and fucking, always fucking. He couldn't get enough of her, on the bed, in the shower, and then he'd wanted to take her again when she'd had her hands in his hair, braiding it. The only thing that had stopped him was the knowledge that they needed to be getting ready for the party and the clean up from all the blood was not a simple task. That was the hazard of what they were, sex was a bloody affair.

His back was marked, permanent scars that showed he had been claimed by a webmaker. She got to bear his scent, he got to bear her scars and he would wear them with pride. He thought of the other men he knew who had similar scars; they must have lost their women at some point. He couldn't imagine losing Aranha, he couldn't imagine going on after her, how had they?

He briefly entertained ideas of locking her in the basement while they went to the party; keeping her safe. He knew it wouldn't work, she'd hate him if he tried to control her like that, but it *was* tempting.

As they left the room and walked out to meet the gathering crowd, he couldn't help putting a possessive arm around her back and pulling her closer. He met Sten's eyes and saw disappointment there. They were closer now, more committed than before and it was obvious to any who were looking. Whatever Sten had hoped for, this wasn't it.

"My sons," Sten said, gathering everyone's attention. "We go tonight to do two things. Save one of our own, and stop the vampires from gaining an ability that doesn't belong to their kind. Our priority is stopping the vampires, everything else is secondary."

Dag roared agreement with his crowd of brothers.

"We fight together, we watch out for each other, and we return together!"

They repeated the pledge that they'd repeated many times in the past, then roared again.

"Time to party!" Sten shouted and the crowd dispersed to vehicles leaving Dag and Aranha looking at Sten.

Sten crossed the distance quickly, a smile pasted on his face. "I see you two are ready." He gave Aranha a look that was full of meaning that Dag didn't understand, but didn't like.

"We are," Aranha said, reaching up and laying a hand on Dag's chest.

"I hope your relationship doesn't inhibit our fight," Sten said, looking at Dag. "Have you reconsidered having her stay behind, it would be safer."

Dag narrowed his eyes, he knew Sten was trying to drive a wedge between them. He felt Aranha stiffen beside him, he tightened his grip on her side. "No, I haven't. She will be invaluable in the fight."

"Wonderful," Sten said stiffly. "See you there." He walked away.

Dag led Aranha to his car and opened the passenger door. Jonah climbed in the back and Aranha took the front. As she settled into the leather seat, he felt a swelling in his body, a warming in his soul and a bursting in his heart. This was his woman, his webmaker, and he was going to do everything possible to bring her back exactly like this.

"What? Do I have blood in my teeth?" she asked with a nervous laugh.

He smiled and shut the door, then walked around the car. "I was just thinking about how I can't wait to encourage you to try and kill me again after we win tonight's battle."

She laughed. "I would love to."

CHAPTER SIXTEEN

THE DRIVE WAS LONG BUT THE SUNSET WAS BEAUTIFUL. They led the way in Dag's car because he was the only technically invited one. When they pulled up to the gate, Aranha couldn't help holding her breath. The werewolf at the gate was the same one who was there the last two mornings, he had caught her scent then, he was going to recognize it now. Panic threatened to overwhelm her.

"Relax, Aranha." Dag said as they waited in a line of cars to be let in.

"He's going to recognize my scent," she whispered harshly. This was a bad idea. She should have gone in as a spider.

Jonah whined in the back.

"You're covered in my scent, no way he'll be able to pick up on yours that easy."

"I hope you're right," she grumbled. They inched closer, now there was only one car in front of them. "Maybe I should shift."

"Your scent would still be here, just relax. If you act like you belong, you're much less likely to be questioned."

She knew he had a point, but her heart was racing. She'd

spent her life avoiding situations where she would have to interact with vampires and werewolves, now here she was, about to party with death.

"What are they going to think of me?" Jonah asked quietly, shrinking back in the seat.

"They are going to think you're my pet, just act like you love me," Dag laughed.

"Yes, sir," Jonah whispered.

"Don't worry, I'll eat him if he even looks at you wrong," Aranha said.

They pulled forward and the bald werewolf leaned down. He was wearing a suit tonight, but he still looked like he could happily brawl with the slightest provocation. His eyes flitted from Dag to Aranha with mild interest, but he caught a whiff of something and his eyes narrowed slightly then shot to the back seat.

"Dag Larsen," Dag said quickly.

"Yeah, I know who you are, who's your lady, what's with the wolf and why is the whole clan following you?"

"Quentin didn't say I couldn't invite anyone," Dag said with a smile. "Now let us through, dog, we are ready to party."

He huffed and stepped back mumbling, "Your funeral."

Dag drove forward and the werewolf waved the other cars through without stopping them.

"That was a little too easy," Dag grumbled.

Aranha looked at him with wide eyes. "You were expecting trouble? Why the hell didn't you say you were expecting not to make it past the fucking gate?"

"I didn't say that, I just thought maybe we would have to bribe him or something."

"So what do you think it means?"

"I think it means that the vampires are very confident in what they have going. Which could be their downfall."

"Or," she prompted.

"Or it could mean we are walking into something unexpected."

"Great, just what I wanted to hear."

"What's life without a little risk for reward, right?" He stopped at the back of the parking area and the others pulled up around them. "This will at least allow for easier escape if needed. Not blocked in by all those cars."

There were a lot of cars in front of them. It worried her greatly. "How many vampires do you think are here tonight?"

"Who knows, but it looks like they came from across the states, a lot of rental plates. They red-eye fly in and rent cars. It can be risky, but so can driving across the country and staying out of sunlight in hotels during the day."

"That one is from Idaho." Aranha pointed to a nearby plate.

"Vampires are all over, and apparently all here."

Dag got out of the car and walked around to her door. She stepped out and Jonah was right behind her. They were immediately surrounded by daywalkers, they were taking their job seriously. The longer she went unnoticed, the better. She would be sifting memories and thoughts as discreetly as she could while in there, but she knew it might not help if she was surrounded by daywalkers too tightly. If she ventured out on her own she was sure to be figured out, and probably killed on the spot. Their plan wasn't without holes.

She was sure they made quite the scene walking. Sten and Dag were in the lead, then there was a row of daywalkers followed by Aranha and Jonah flanked on both sides by two daywalkers and behind her were two more rows of daywalkers. It was like a very odd military procession and she felt ridiculous, but she also felt safe and cared for.

At the door there were two werewolves standing guard. They didn't stop or question them, just opened the doors and let them in. They did look questioningly at Jonah, but they didn't comment.

"Brought your own dinner to a dinner party?" One of them commented as she passed. Four daywalkers hissed in his direction, immediately deflecting all concern over her presence. Aranha felt like a princess, or a prize racehorse at the very least.

She'd never been in this door or seen the rooms up front that they were walking through. It was beautiful in its gothic Victorian style, she wasn't surprised. What did surprise her, were the number of obvious humans roaming the place. Not just the seven prostitutes that she was expecting. She did spot one or two of them immediately, but there were others and they looked completely voluntary.

"Human pets?" she whispered.

"Yeah, many vampires have a willing human with them, especially when they travel." The daywalker beside her answered. She wasn't sure of his name but she thought she remembered it started with a C.

"Gross, why would they do that?"

"They want to be turned, most often they die. It's not easy to turn someone, which is why they want to resurrect Eve, obviously."

Aranha knew that bit of trivia. She looked around the large room of conversing vampires, human pets, prostitutes and werewolves with disgust. This was not the world she was a part of, this is what she was born to stop. She spread a bit of web between her fingers, trying to be discreet. As expected, she was only picking up thoughts from the daywalkers around her, and some of those she seriously wished she'd not heard. Too many involved her in some form of undress.

She quickly crushed it with a sigh.

"What's wrong?"

"Calder?" She asked, she really didn't want to be rude since he insisted on talking to her as they moved farther into the room.

"Yeah."

"Just can't get a read because of all you guys so close. I'm not sure I can do any good unless I venture out a bit."

"Not allowed," he said sternly.

She hissed at him and her hand went to her belt where she knew a blade rested, she didn't do well with *allowed*. Dag shot a deadly look at Calder. "It's fine," she whispered and took a breath.

Calder gave a little huff of laughter. "He's protective,"

"Yeah," she agreed happily.

The crowd watched them, but mostly kept chatting. Wine was flowing and there was even food for the eaters. It was a nice little party if you ignored the fact that there was a good chance Lars was about to be sacrificed and a girl possibly possessed.

A man was sitting on a throne in one corner and as the crowd parted a little more, it became clear he was sitting on a piece of raised floor, like a true king. This was no doubt, Quentin Russell. He was surprisingly old, his long hair was grey, his face wrinkled; but his eyes were a deep dark brown and they were not in the slightest hazy. He may have been turned as an old man, but he was sharp as ever mentally. He was wearing a purple velvet smoking jacket and black button up shirt. His pants were black pinstripe and his shoes a shiny white patent leather.

He was flanked by vampires who looked much younger and bared their fangs at Dag and Sten as they approached. Quentin raised a hand and they quieted immediately, so did the rest of the crowd. Aranha wished she could have looked around to see what was going on but she had to keep her eyes down, out of sight.

"Dag, so glad you could make it. I see you brought your whole clan."

"I didn't think it would be right to keep them from a party, especially since you already had one clan member here."

Quentin laughed. "Lars, yes, he will be joining us shortly. You have a female," he said quietly, and his eyes narrowed on Aranha.

She kept her eyes down and it took everything she had to do it, it went against everything in her to show submission. If he got a good look at her eyes, he would know. They all would. Calder touched her arm lightly, offering comfort or reminding her to keep her head down, she wasn't sure.

"Yes, my girlfriend. I thought it would be fun to bring her to see your grand party."

"Dag has a human pet? I am shocked, I thought you weren't into relationships."

"I'm not, it's just about sex."

Quentin laughed, apparently accepting this explanation. "The young wolf? Where did he come from and how did he get mixed in with your kind?"

"I found him alone in the city and offered him safety," Dag offered as explanation.

"Interesting... Well, you are all welcome to stay for the show. I don't expect any trouble, of course we are well equipped to handle it if you guys get out of hand." Quentin motioned around the room and there were answering growls from a dozen werewolves.

Shit! Was all she could think, this was more than she'd bargained for. Had anyone else expected twelve or more werewolves plus thirty or more vampires, not to mention their humans? Against their twenty-five! The odds weren't good. Jonah was shaking slightly beside her, the energy in the room was intense.

"Thank you for your hospitality," Dag said, and turned away. Their group moved and broke apart as if they knew exactly what to do. She didn't, so she stood with Calder, Jonah, and another daywalker by her side until Dag was there and grabbing her arm. Then they moved away from Quentin, a tight group of five while the others positioned themselves around the room in apparent randomness that Aranha very much doubted was random.

"That went well," she whispered.

"Better than expected. Their confidence though is disturbing," Dag grumbled.

"Can we use it against them, they don't expect us to be able to do anything and they don't think we know about Evelyn."

"I think that's the only thing we have going for us right now. Do you know where she is?"

"No, I couldn't see that, but I know where Lars is."

"I don't think we should go after him unless we can get her out too. Can you try and pick up some thoughts?"

"Yeah, now that I'm not surrounded by daywalkers I should be able to get something else, their thoughts were loud."

Dag hissed and Calder stepped back, hands up. "Not me, man. I have no interest in her."

Aranha laughed. "Chill Dag, thoughts are often no indication of what a person can and will do. Trust me, I can tell the difference between passing curiosity and evil intention."

"No one should be thinking about you."

"Yeah, well, get over it."

Calder laughed and gained a glare from Dag. "She's not wrong man, you know your brothers are curious, but it's not as if any one of them would entertain the thought of taking your marked woman. Some of us are old enough to have loved and lost." Calder's voice cracked and Aranha couldn't help reaching out to offer a comforting hand on his arm. He gave her an appreciative smile. "It's a deep pain that never really goes away."

Dag grumbled but didn't continue to hiss at his brother. They had positioned themselves toward the entrance with a good view of the room and a large distance between themselves and Quentin. Aranha stepped away from the group slightly and spread a web between her fingers.

She was inundated with thoughts and memories. A large gathering like this was overwhelming. First she sifted through the humans, they were useless. Most were filled with some level of terror, willing victims or not, they were all afraid. Afraid that they would die, afraid that they would be left or forgotten, traded perhaps to a vampire that wasn't as nice, cute, or rich. They were afraid that they were making a mistake, that they had rushed into this in a fit of depression and would regret the decision to become immortal. A few were just afraid. The prostitutes who hadn't chosen to be here barely understood the reality they were in, but they were too smart to try and run. They thought if they played the game they would be paid and let go; that's what they had been told when they woke up after being drugged and kidnapped. They were working very hard to keep the knowledge of all the girls they'd seen disappear in a van and never return, out of their minds. This couldn't be that situation, that was something else entirely... surely.

Aranha felt sorry for them and hoped she could save them, but knew she may not be able to save them all and that bothered her. She allowed the humans to flow through without sticking, they were useless and more than a little depressing.

The werewolves were angry, their thoughts and memories were always wrapped up in emotions. Tonight they all seemed on edge and unsure. None of them were thinking about anything helpful though. They were analyzing and watching, especially aware of the daywalkers, and her. *Shit*, they were very interested in why she smelled different.

"The werewolves smell me," she whispered to Dag, moving closer.

She was instantly surrounded by daywalkers, casually moving into a protective circle position.

"What do they think?"

"They don't know what I am, but they don't seem to think I'm human."

"Then the clock is ticking. It's likely they've never even heard of webmakers, werewolves don't tend to live long lives. They might think you are something different but they shouldn't be able to place you. What about the vampires?" Dag whispered, his voice full of worry.

Aranha dug through the vampire thoughts and memories she'd caught. "Most don't know why they are here. They have lots of theories but don't know why the summons came. They are concentrating on Quentin and ignoring us and the werewolves."

"Quentin wants to make a big show, that's not surprising," Calder said.

Aranha continued to search. "Those who know are doubtful, they don't all think it will work but there is a lot of hope too. This feels like a last-ditch effort of survival, there's a general sense of concern among those who know. They think perhaps Quentin has lost his hold on reality and if things don't go as he plans, he may destroy them all."

"We need to know more about the plan itself."

"They aren't thinking in particulars, I'm not a damn mind reader," Aranha hissed. "Who's Quentin's closest advisor? Get me close but keep him distracted."

Dag looked at one of the daywalkers surrounding her.

"Fiske," he said, and the man hurried off to stand beside a woman, a vampire, and started up a conversation.

She was dressed in a floor length red silk dress that hugged her slender curves and was cut so wide you could see the curves of her breasts and Aranha was sure there was tape there holding her nipples behind the thin fabric. She was stunning. Long blonde hair curled around her shoulders and she had deep green eyes. Her face showed no reaction or emotion to Fiske, but she didn't shoo him away either.

"Ella is Quentin's partner and confidant. She'll know everything and she has the tendency to sleep with daywalkers, so Fiske will keep her well distracted."

"Gross, but okay move me close."

Dag pulled her close and hissed playfully. "What do you mean gross?" He kissed her deeply, leaving her feeling a little breathless and weak-kneed.

"What?" she whispered as he pulled away.

"You think sleeping with daywalkers is gross?" he whispered.

"I think sleeping with a vampire is gross, I mean, they're dead, can they even..."

Calder laughed beside them. Dag gave her a sardonic look. "They aren't dead, they're transformed and yes they can."

"Gross, but alright, get me close."

Their little group moved to the other side of the room where Fiske was apprising Ella of all the beautiful things about her. She was eating it up and completely ignoring the rest of the room.

Aranha stepped away from the others just enough to get a clear flow from Ella, she wasn't disappointed, Ella's thoughts were loud and clear, and sexual.

"This won't work, unless she stops thinking about Fiske naked," Aranha whispered.

As if on cue, Fiske guided her thoughts. "So can we step away, I mean this party is kind of boring compared to what we could get up to in your room."

Ella giggled and frowned. "Sorry, Fiske baby, can't leave yet, the show is about to start."

Aranha got a clear picture there. Lars flayed open on the stage, a pile of bones, fire, and Evelyn, in a white gown.

"What kind of show could be better than the one I'll give you?" Fiske pressed.

"If I told you, I'd have to kill you," she let her fangs extend as she smiled. "Don't worry, we will begin very soon. If you're still standing when it's over, I will take you up on the romp, you know I'm always down for a little time with you."

Her thoughts were back to the bedroom and Aranha crushed the web, she didn't need to see those memories. "Fiske likes it rough," she groaned as she returned to her safe group.

"Yeah, no surprise there," Calder said with a laugh.

"Anything worthwhile?" Dag asked.

"Still don't know where the girl is currently, but there is something about Lars, the girl and some bones. Lars seemed imperative to the whole thing. Are you sure it was coincidental that he was captured?"

Dag gave her a slight shrug. "I think they were after me, honestly, or why would they have been outside my condo building. I'm no special breed and if they took Lars instead, it must not have mattered, they just need a daywalker sacrifice."

Aranha wasn't convinced. There was something they didn't know about Lars, she was sure.

CHAPTER SEVENTEEN

"I want to go talk to Lars," she whispered to Dag as he pulled her back to a corner.

"No."

"I think we should know what he knows," she argued, this was not going to be a relationship where he dominated her every move, except maybe in the bedroom, she was pretty sure she could go along with that.

"Even if it didn't include you being naked in front of him again, it's too risky, we don't want them to know what you are, at least not yet."

"I could go," Jonah whispered.

"No!" Dag and Aranha hissed in unison.

Jonah pouted but didn't argue.

Calder gave Jonah a pat on the shoulder. "Don't worry, brother, I bet you'll get a chance to be useful soon enough. Your teeth will rip apart a vampire nice and quick when it comes to a fight."

Aranha frowned at Calder, she didn't like the idea of Jonah in a fight. "Get me close to Quentin," she told Dag.

"I don't think it matters at this point."

Aranha followed Dag's gaze to Quentin's stage. He was standing now and everyone was looking at him expectantly.

"Let the show begin," Calder said beside them.

Dag put an arm around her waist and pulled her close to his side. She instinctively wanted to brush off the show of protection, but she didn't move away. She liked that he cared, and one hand rested close to her knife reminding her that she wasn't helpless.

"My gathered friends," Quentin began. "I know that you are all quite curious as to why we are all gathered here tonight. Well, let me first tell you a little story. Some of you will recognize it, some will not. Know this! It is the truth as I know it and I just might be the oldest thing in this room."

"Is he?" She whispered to Dag.

"Could be, I know he's older than Sten who is one of the oldest daywalkers I've ever met."

"Is that why he's in charge?"

"Sten or Quentin?"

"Both."

"Yes, with age comes power and they have both lived through a hell of a lot to get to where they are," Dag assured her.

"There was a garden at the beginning of time," Sten began. "A garden where two supposedly perfect beings were meant to live, thrive, and populate, I think you will all recognize that story."

There was a murmur of agreement throughout the room.

"Those two beings were Adam, the daywalker and Eve, the webmaker. They lived in the garden, but what did they eat? Neither beast was made to live off the land, so something else was created. Food for their particular appetites. Humans were given to Adam and Eve for sustenance. The two thrived in the garden and had children. Female children were born webmakers like their mother, male children, daywalkers." He paused here and smiled at the crowd. "Would you like to believe that they then mated with their siblings? While I am a fan of all sorts of debauchery, I still find this a hard fact to swallow. So they looked to the humans, they had all the same parts, they were just a little more... delicate. What they bore were some children like them, daywalkers and webmakers with lessened powers, some simply human. Others were unexpected, children who craved blood like their fathers but couldn't stand in the sun. Children who shifted like their mothers, but into huge beasts controlled by the moon!"

Quentin's insinuation that vampires and werewolves were created by daywalkers and webmakers breeding with humans was shocking to Aranha. Beside her Dag looked just as confused.

"Adam and Eve found these beings to be abominations! They were cast out of the garden as if they were trash, barren and destined to be alone in the darkness of earth among animals. The gods were ashamed of the actions of their two chosen ones, they took pity on the children and sent humans to live by their sides, providing nutrition to the vampires, and company to the werewolves. Before the humans left, they were tricked by Adam and Eve into eating from the tree; their memories of the garden stripped so that they would only see the vampires and werewolves who were their kin, as fearsome terrible beasts! When the gods discovered this trickery had been done, they banished the daywalkers and webmakers from the garden, and stripped them of their abilities to breed with the humans who would now instinctively fear them as well. With one last parting shot, Eve took something from the garden into her body, the birthing water from which Adam and she were born from the earth. In this water lies the ability to give us what we have always deserved. The ability to breed! To create in our own image, not just turn humans."

Aranha's jaw was hanging as she tried to understand all of what he had just said.

"What the fuck?" Dag said beside her.

Quentin stood looking very proud of himself, arms crossed over his chest, watching the crowd react.

"Why do we need to breed?" someone shouted.

"Oh simpleton, how do you not see? It is the only thing that keeps us from taking our place. You see, we are the ultimate! We are the strongest, the smartest, and we deserve to have our time. If it should have been any other way, it would have by now. We wiped out the webmakers, made a peace with the few remaining daywalkers, but they do not control us. Humans abound, humans are everywhere acting as if they are the top. We are! They were never meant to be anything but food! We would have ruled the garden given a chance and that is why they threw us out first. They were afraid, and they should have been." Quentin looked right at Sten as he spoke his next words. "Once we have the ability to breed more of ourselves, we will be unstoppable and everyone else will be dog food."

On cue the werewolves growled around the room.

"Why are the werewolves going along with this?" Aranha whispered to Dag. She was frightened more than ever, this man was insane to another level and whatever he was planning to try and do was going to be difficult to stop.

"I don't know, probably just happy to be second to the king. It's not a bad place to be, all the rewards, not all the headaches."

"So now you know the problem," Quentin continued when the room settled. "What solution do I offer?" He asked rhetorically to the crowd, which answered with whoops of agreement. "Vlad, the box."

A huge vampire came forward with a large gold and black enamel box in his arms. He was a big man, and the box was almost too large for him to carry comfortably it seemed.

"Evelyn?" Aranha whispered to herself, hoping she was wrong. If the girl was in there, she was not likely to be alive still.

"I am glad that you are all here to bear witness to tonight's revelations. It will do us well to have our message of triumph spread quickly throughout the immortal community. In this box," Quentin smiled and rubbed his hands together like a child about to open a present. Vlad set the box on a table next to Quentin's throne. "In this box are the bones of our beloved first mother. The original birther. Eve."

A gasp went up in the room, no one outside of Quentin's circle knew about this, it seemed.

Quentin was visibly vibrating with excitement as he lifted the lid on the box. He tilted it slightly to appease the crowd, which was now pushing forward for a better view, all except for the daywalkers. From where she stood, Aranha could see that the box was lined with red velvet and there were indeed bones inside. They looked old, discolored and dirty, but there was no telling whose they were, not really.

"These are from the tomb in Jeddah and they will serve as the catalyst for calling Eve's spirit forth. Two other things are required for the ceremony. Birth water from the garden, and a vessel to hold her soul."

"How the fuck does he think he has the water? That's not even possible, right?" Aranha asked Dag who just looked forward with disbelief and anger on his face—that was not reassuring.

"He certainly *thinks* he has it," Calder said.

"One more part to this story." Quentin began again. "When Eve left with the water in her body, she was pregnant. This was her last child and it is my belief, that in the blood of this child resides the water." Quentin raised a hand and Lars was led into the room in chains.

"Eve's last son," Quentin announced.

Lars was shirtless, his pants bloody and ripped. He looked like he'd been beat up pretty badly but his head was high. There was a chain around his neck, wrists, and ankles. She could see the skin was burning where it touched, silver no doubt. The chains were held by a vampire wearing gloves to protect his own skin. Aranha wanted to rush forward, wanted to pull out her blades. She knew she could hit that vampire between the eyes. It might not kill him, but it would certainly distract him long enough for someone else to jump in and rip out his throat.

Dag's hand was on her arm, steadying her. She looked up at his face and he shook his head slightly. "Not yet," he whispered so low she wasn't sure she heard him. There was a hush in the room as Lars was led to the stage.

"Are you, Lars, the last son born of Adam and Eve? Conceived in the garden?"

The silence became even deeper, not a finger rustled, not a breath was released.

"I am," Lars said and there was a collective intake of breath as everyone tried to calculate his age at the same time as they tried to comprehend how Quentin's plan might actually work.

"Your blood will spill for us tonight," Quentin said with satisfaction.

Aranha saw Fiske take a step toward his brother, but Sten was quick to stop him. From across the room, a simple raised hand stopped Fiske from going farther. Aranha hoped they had a plan because this was getting progressively more fucked, in her mind.

"And now the vessel, a beautiful young human to hold the soul and drink the blood. She will become a vampire and she *will* hold the ability to breed."

A roar of approval went up through the crowd.

Lars' eyes met hers across the room. There was a message there she couldn't quite grasp. "Get me near Lars," she told Dag.

He looked at her, clearly wanting to deny at first. She narrowed her eyes, this was no time to get cold feet. They were there to fight, to stop this insanity and save the girl at all costs.

Dag pushed her around the gathered crowd, to the side of the stage where Fiske stood, Elle had left the room, to gather the girl presumably. The crowd was busily congratulating Quentin on his genius.

"I hope you have a damn good plan," Fiske hissed at Dag.

"Yep, and she's right here," Dag hissed back, pushing Aranha forward.

Aranha spread a web between her fingers and tried to pinpoint Lars' thoughts in the crowd. There were so many loud thoughts, it was difficult—so much excitement, lust, and jealousy. Aranha was sure that if the girl became a breedable vampire, she'd be torn apart by those who would try and control her. She'd not survive the night among these monsters.

Then she caught it, Lars' thoughts were shouting out to her. *Kill me, take my blood, so the girl cannot.*

She met his gaze, her mouth wide. She shook her head, no way could she do that, it was insane.

It's the only way to save her, she must not take my blood. When they enter the room, they will be distracted. I am a willing sacrifice, you can't imagine how long I've walked this earth, what I have seen... I am tired, and I am ready. His mind went quiet, he closed his eyes, and she got a picture of something beautiful; complete relaxation and what she could only describe as Zen. He really was at peace with this decision, and he really did think it was the only way.

She just wasn't sure she was capable. She wasn't a blood drinker except in the smallest amounts. She was confident she could do some damage, take in a liter maybe, but not quickly, not before Quentin or one of his lackeys stepped in to stop her.

She froze, Dag could, Calder and Fiske could. Together

they could drain him faster than anyone could react, but would they? This was their brother.

She looked at Dag. "I know what we have to do."

Dag raised an eyebrow. "Start killing everyone?" He said darkly.

"We have to drain Lars, his blood cannot be used for the ceremony and he is ready to move on from this earth."

"I—" Dag started, then froze, eyes lifting to Lars. Lars was looking at him and nodded slightly. "Shit." Dag groaned.

"I think we could drain him fast enough with Fiske and Calder's help. Jonah, stand guard," she ordered.

Jonah gave her a fearful look but nodded. He'd been behind her, trying to stay close and hidden, she needed him to find some courage now.

A flurry of activity drew everyone's attention to the back of the room. Aranha couldn't see, but she was sure it was Elle with the girl. Now was the time. "We have to do it now, it's Lars or the girl and you know Lars would not choose her to die."

Dag turned to his two brothers and gave quick harsh instructions. As the crowd parted and Evelyn was led forward, all eyes were on her. Aranha moved, swift and sure, she could feel the others follow. They descended on their friend and brother who had moved as close as he could to their side of the stage. Lars spread his arms, closed his eyes, and let his head fall back. His sacrifice was willing and she hoped, not in vain.

Aranha went for the soft exposed neck. She closed her eyes, fangs out, she pierced his skin and drank. Fast and deep and hard, taking in as much as her small body could handle. She knew she might puke it up later, her body wasn't meant to handle much pure blood and she'd already taken some from Dag tonight.

Screams erupted around her almost instantly.

Aranha was grabbed from behind and instinctively she

shifted and managed to crawl quickly out of her falling dress and onto Lars. Now a small spider on Lars' neck she scrambled for cover. Hands scooped her up as Lars' body fell lifeless. There was chaos all around, screaming and fighting. The hands closed around her, she shifted back to human form. Naked and sprawled on the floor, she stared up at the glaring eyes of Quentin.

Jonah shifted and attacked Quentin. He was a small blond wolf, but he was still dangerous. He latched onto Quentin's arm and shook his head, ripping clothes and drawing blood.

Quentin reacted fast, grabbing him by the scruff and throwing him off. Jonah hit a wall and slumped to the floor. Aranha wanted to scream and go after him, but she wouldn't dare turn her back on Quentin.

"Webmaker! How the hell do you exist?"

"Yeah, not sorry," she hissed and scrambled away until her back hit the wall. Her eyes darted around as Quentin stalked forward. She couldn't see Dag anywhere and her weapons were in her pile of clothing she'd vacated. All around there were hisses, growls and the sounds of breaking bones and clashing steel. She didn't dare risk looking away from Quentin to assess who was winning.

"You have the blood, don't think I can't rip it out of your stomach."

"Just try," she hissed and crouched, she would rather die than let him go through with this insanity.

She was so focused on Quentin, she missed the movement beside her. A chain whipped out and around her body, her instincts were to shift and scramble, but she couldn't! Her eyes widened on the vampire Elle next to her.

"What is this?"

"Enhanced silver chain. It's one way we so quickly took out

the webmakers, how the hell you slipped through, I have no idea," she sneered.

Aranha tried again, nothing happened, she was helpless unless they got close enough to bite. She bared her fangs at the woman and hissed.

"Feisty, I like that," Quentin laughed. He leaned down and grabbed a handful of her hair, forcing her forward on her knees.

She was now kneeling next to the bones, looking out on a crowd that was pulsing in battle. She still couldn't see Dag, was he already dead? Did she want to survive this if he didn't?

Quentin pulled out a knife. A flash of blond fur—Jonah was back up—rammed into Quentin in time to deflect the blade. It sliced across Aranha's stomach as intended, but not as deep. The pain was still sharp though, and she screamed.

Quentin turned and jumped at Jonah, his knife lashing out at him.

Blackness surrounded Aranha as she fell and the last thing she knew was the face of Evelyn above her. Just before she gave herself over to the blackness of what must be death, she saw a spider on the girl's shoulder and Aranha smiled. Maybe the girl would be okay.

CHAPTER EIGHTEEN

Dag was injured. He'd caught a sword to the side as he'd drained Lars. Then Aranha had disappeared and he was thrown out into a fighting crowd. He had to turn off the fear that was consuming him as he fought alongside his brothers. Wherever she was, he would get to her, and he would save her, but on the way he would take out as many bloodsuckers and dogs as he could.

The humans were a nuisance in the middle of battle, screaming and carrying on like they were on fire in the middle of an oil field. He pushed more than one of them harshly to the ground as they got between him and his next goal. He ripped into the throats of three vampires and one werewolf before managing to reach the stage again.

He froze when he saw her lifeless naked body, her stomach slashed open and her eyes closed. Quentin was lashing out now at a blond wolf that must have been Jonah. The girl, Evelyn he assumed, was standing there in a white gown, hands reaching out, a fierce look in her eyes and hundreds of spiders rushing forward around her.

Dag had no idea where they were coming from or why the human girl wasn't afraid, but he knew what this was.

This was the hellfire fury of Eve.

Windows exploded around the room and women dressed in battle gear swarmed. Men were flung across the room wrapped in webs and Dag had no idea if the daywalkers were enemies of them or not, but it didn't matter, all that mattered in that moment was vengeance for Aranha.

"What the hell have you done?" Dag hissed at Quentin as he leaped for the vampire. Jonah stepped back, allowing Dag to take on this enemy. Dag caught Quentin at the knees, taking him down to the floor. He scrambled up and his hand went to Quentin's throat and squeezed. The vampire's eyes bulged, and his hands clawed at Dag's hold, his hips bucked, and his feet pushed, but he couldn't budge Dag, not when Dag had the blood of his brother flowing through his body and the fury of his lost love in his soul.

Dag smiled as he squeezed harder and he saw the recognition of death in Quentin's eyes. "No one is coming to save you. You miscalculated what power you were dealing with. Eve would never let your abomination take more from the world, she's sent her warriors and I am going to squash you like the vermin you are."

Dag finished him; quick and not as painfully as he would have liked. He ripped out his throat, then pulled his head from his body to be certain he didn't regenerate.

"That death was too good for you," he spat at the body as he stood. If he'd had time, he would have made the monster suffer for perhaps years before giving him the ultimate release of death. The punishment for Aranha's death should have been so much more. He spit on Quentin's body, "I hope you're in hell."

Dag looked around and saw that the fighting was almost done. The humans had run, probably most of the werewolves too. Vampire parts were strewn across the room and there were dozens of webmakers holding the daywalkers at sword points, both sides unsure where they stood with the other. Spiders were everywhere and Dag wasn't sure if they were webmakers unwilling to shift and be nude, or perhaps just pets.

"Help her," he croaked to no one in particular and fell beside Aranha, tears flowing freely, not caring what anyone thought of him. "If you have any ability, you have to help her." There were webmakers here, he wasn't sure how, but they were and if they'd survived the extinction of their species perhaps, they could do something for Aranha that he couldn't.

Jonah crawled forward, whining, and laid next to Aranha, licking her face.

Dag felt a hand on his shoulder and he looked up into the face of a webmaker. She was dressed in leather pants and corset, her black hair cut short. There was a long scar on the right side of her face and she was frowning. Her black eyes sad as they looked from him to Aranha.

"She is gone to the garden, she is with the true mother now."

"No! She can't be gone, I just found her! If she is somewhere she can come back," Dag reasoned.

"Her heart has stopped, I know you can feel that," the woman persisted. "I am Enya, leader of the webmakers."

"I don't believe you."

"You don't believe that I am leader here?" she scoffed.

"I don't believe that she can't come back. She took a lot of blood, her body is still warm. She can come back!"

"There is a way." A spider shifted to human form next to Enya. At least some of the spiders were webmakers and the implications of such a large clan was not something he could comprehend at the moment.

Dag had so many questions, but none of the answers mattered if Aranha was gone. "How?" he demanded.

"Thekla, you can't—"

"I can and I will, don't you see what is happening here? How long has it been since our kinds were able to find love? This is our chance for redemption and reunion." Thekla spoke slow and sure, stepping forward and touching Enya's shoulder. "We have to try."

"Please, if there is even a chance."

"It would take the power of your blood," Enya explained.

"Do it," Dag demanded, holding out his arm. "Take whatever you need."

"She will also have to choose coming back," Enya said sternly.

"She's mine, fucking do it!"

Jonah growled agreement.

Enya stepped back and gathered the bones of Eve. Dag looked around the room. The survivors no longer looked like they were mid battle; they were all gathered close, watching with varying degrees of shock and interest. Enya brought the bones close to Aranha's body. Dag held Aranha's hand and kissed her lips, they were still warm. Evelyn, knelt next to Aranha, one hand resting on Aranha's heart, the other on the bones of Eve.

Aranha was floating, she knew that she was dying, knew that her body was lost but somehow holding on. Like a rope was still attached but thinning and she was getting closer and closer to something else, something beautiful and peaceful.

It started to appear before her slowly, the outlines of trees and bushes, a waterfall and pond. There were people too, she could see their outlines. Behind her, she could hear voices. She knew Dag was there, but she couldn't tell what he was saying, she couldn't turn to look at them, and she wasn't sure she wanted to.

The picture before her sharpened. The water was a brilliant blue, sparkling in the sunlight and so inviting. The trees were the brightest green she'd ever seen and the bushes were covered in every color blossom one could imagine. It was paradise. Animals moved about, unafraid and watching. The people were all nude and unashamed, wearing welcoming smiles. She felt like she was coming home.

A woman stepped forward and Aranha recognized her immediately. "Mother!" she cried out and tried to move toward her faster but she couldn't. She was still tied to her body, still tethered to earth somehow.

"My darling, Aranha! I have waited years to see you, but it's too soon, what trouble has befallen you?"

"I've been so lonely! I am so sorry, it was all my fault that they found you," she cried, arms reaching out to her mother. She wanted nothing more than to be welcomed into those familiar arms.

"No child, it was hate that killed me. *You* are love." Her smile was bright and full of love that made Aranha ache.

Aranha felt tears fall down her cheeks, she couldn't get there fast enough, she was ready for this, ready to be with her mother again. "I'm coming," she said, and strained forward but she didn't move any faster.

Another woman moved beside her mother and put an arm around Carinen's shoulder. They shared a meaningful look and the new woman whispered in her ear. Carinen turned to look at Aranha with a new sadness.

"Your time is not up. Your lover calls to you, there is much more you can do outside of the garden."

"It's hard down there, life is... *hard*," Aranha cried. She felt like a toddler; she wanted her mother and the comfort of her arms, nothing else could compete with that desire.

"It's okay, you'll join us someday, but not today. Eve is being called forth by her daughters, your sisters. Go together and heal the clans, it is your destiny."

The woman who'd approached Carinen started to float toward Aranha. She was holding her arms out to her and there was a smile on her face. She looked young, but her eyes were deep with knowledge. When their hands touched, Aranha felt a calmness spread over her.

"We have much work to do, Aranha," she said softly.

"I don't want any responsibilities, I never asked for that."

"Your life will always be your own. I just ask that you help heal, remind them of the love we once shared together."

"And when I die, I'll go back there, to the garden?" Aranha already felt herself being pulled away from it, back to earth, back to her body and Dag. Back to pain and suffering.

"Yes, all my children go there when they leave the earth."

Aranha wasn't sure if she understood it all; but if she would be with her mother in paradise again someday, then having more time with Dag on earth was impossible to turn down. She hadn't spent nearly enough time getting to know the way their bodies could interact. And Jonah! He needed her still.

Aranha opened her eyes suddenly and looked up at Dag's relieved face.

"For fuck's sake, Aranha, are you okay?"

"No," she groaned. Everything hurt and she wasn't sure what was real in this moment.

Dag laughed. "Don't move, let Thekla look you over."

Aranha felt a tongue lick her face. "Gross, Jonah!"

He whined and licked her again.

"I'm fine, I'm fine."

A woman was there on the other side of her, nude and not caring one bit. Aranha realized she was still quite exposed. As if reading her mind, Dag took off his jacket and covered her bottom half. The woman was pressing her hands to Aranha's stomach and it hurt. "What the hell are you doing?" she snapped.

"The wound has closed, but you'll need some time to fully heal. No activity, rest," she said, more to Dag than Aranha.

Thekla moved away and shifted to spider. Another woman, this one clothed for battle, stepped forward. Dag slipped the coat further up, covering her fully. "I am Enya, leader of the webmakers. I had no idea you existed. I would have come for you before now, I apologize. You've been alone for a long time it seems." Enya took Aranha's hand gently and looked into her eyes with a deep sorrow. "I can't even imagine what it must have been like without your sisters. We are here now though, we will care for you."

"She's not going anywhere with you!" Dag hissed.

"We can care for her, *daywalker*," Enya hissed back.

"I am not her enemy," Dag bared his teeth at her, threatening.

"Yet she lies here almost dead because of you," Enya accused.

"No," Aranha said, trying to sit up. That was a mistake, she fell back down immediately, groaning with pain. It felt like her abdomen was shredded.

"Don't move, love, we will figure out a safe way to transport you home," Dag said softly.

Aranha laughed at the word home, she couldn't help it, there was no such place for her, hadn't ever been. "Where's that?"

"We'll stay at the compound until you heal, then back to the city, to my condo. You know it's safe there."

"She should be with her kind, she should come with us," Enya insisted.

Jonah whined beside her, looking from Dag to Enya.

"And where is that?" Dag hissed. "You know she can't move far, she will go to the compound and she will be safe to heal."

They glared at each other and Aranha rolled her eyes at their ridiculousness.

"Why don't we stay here? I can't move far like this, I think I need some sleep. Maybe tomorrow we can make it to the compound or the city." She tried to make her stance clear, she was staying with Dag.

"Fine, but we are staying too," Enya said firmly.

"Of course!" Sten said, stepping forward from the crowd. "I am Sten, leader of the daywalkers."

"Yes, we know who you are," Enya said, with a look that showed she was far from impressed.

Dag looked into Aranha's eyes and there was a deep worry there. "I will make this as painless as possible," he promised.

Aranha just nodded.

"Calder, Fiske, help me carry her to the nearest room with a bed." The two men came forward and together the three slipped hands under her body and lifted in unison.

Aranha bit her lip to keep from screaming out in pain and sweat beaded on her brow with the effort. She didn't make it all the way to the bed, the pain was too much and her mind went blissfully black.

CHAPTER NINETEEN

Aranha wasn't sure how long she'd slept, but when she awoke, the sky was bright and she was alone. She could hear voices not far away though, so she didn't think she'd be alone very long. Aranha lifted the blanket and peered down at her stomach. Still tender and there was a large pink scar, but it wasn't as bad as last night—she was healing. She tried to sit up, and that was a mistake.

"Fuck," Aranha groaned, falling back down.

The bedroom door opened and Dag hurried in. "Are you okay?"

"Yeah, I think so. How long have I been out?"

"About twelve hours, you needed it."

"Where's Jonah?"

Dag laughed. "Well, he found a cute little webmaker that he's been spending a lot of time with."

"No!" Aranha was shocked, and so happy.

"Yep, adorable thing, her name is Evelyn."

"Wait... you don't mean?"

"Yeah, you didn't come back alone, apparently the girl was primed enough to take on Eve's spirit and when you escaped back from the garden she came too. Turned her into a webmaker as a result."

"Is she okay?"

"She is, so far. I guess it's best because she couldn't exactly go back to her human life, right? At least she isn't a vampire."

Dag looked around the room. "The webmakers haven't left you alone, no matter how many times I've asked them to go away and wait for me to tell them you're awake. I'm surprised we're alone now."

"Nothing wrong with a little concern."

"I think there's something more." His face grew concerned and his hands fisted. "I think they want to convince you to go with them."

"Yeah, they probably do," she agreed with a sigh.

Dag pulled a chair close to the bed and leaned down to kiss her gently. "Are you hungry?"

"No, I'm fine. How are things going, with everyone together?"

"The webmakers have lived a long time in hiding. I don't think they remember how it was when we were all together."

"What brought them here?"

"We sensed Eve. Her bones were taken from their resting place and we followed, and we watched." Enya had come into the room followed by Thekla.

Dag looked at the two women and sighed heavily. "She just woke up, I didn't have time to alert you yet."

"I know, I sensed her rousing so I came to check," Enya said, nonchalant as she crossed the room, and laid a hand on Aranha's arm. "How are you feeling, dear?"

"Definitely better but still a little tender."

"You won't be doing crunches any time soon," Enya laughed.

"Let me take a look," Thekla said and pulled down the

blanket without waiting for permission. She poked deep and made Aranha squirm, but she didn't cry out.

"Is that necessary?" Dag asked between clenched teeth.

"If we can't see it, we have to feel it, or we don't know it's healing," Thekla said, covering Aranha back up. She smiled into Aranha's face. "I think you are healing well, you should probably try and walk a bit today if you can."

"Thank you, for everything," Aranha said. She was truly happy to be here and to see concern on Dag's face. Knowing he cared meant a lot. She missed her mother, but she knew she would have missed him more. This is where she wanted to be.

"I'm so sorry I couldn't prevent this hurt," Dag whispered.

"I'm glad you didn't let me go," she whispered back and she could feel emotion building in her throat and tears stinging her eyes. "My feelings for you... feel about the same as before, I assure you."

He smiled and gave her a light kiss.

"Now, you let her rest. I'll check back in with you in a bit." Thekla ordered, then she and Enya left.

Aranha reached up and touched Dag's cheek. "I could have stayed, my mother was there."

Dag's eyes widened and he inhaled sharply. "You saw her in the garden and you returned?"

"Yeah, it's beautiful, Dag, and I can't wait to be there someday with my mother and... and you, perhaps. Unless we get sick of each other before then," she laughed.

"Why did you choose this? Earth is so..."

"Painful?"

"Yeah."

"Because I want more of you, of us. If this had happened before I met you, nothing could have made me leave the garden. You are worth the pain, Dag. I want to experience life with you."

Dag cupped her face and leaned down, touching her lips lightly. "I don't want to hurt you, but as soon as you are able, I am going to show you how much I want you, forever."

His promise made her heart skip a beat and she smiled at him. "I can't wait to let you do just that."

"Now rest," he commanded gently.

She stuck her tongue out at him, but she closed her eyes. She wanted to heal fast and she knew sleep would help.

Dag left when he thought she was asleep and a few moments later, Jonah crept in and laid beside her on the bed. She wrapped her arms around him and his whole body shuddered as he cried.

"I thought I was going to lose you."

"No way, I'm way tough and I know you protected me," she whispered against his head.

"I tried."

"You did a good job, Jonah, you're a good boy."

He snuggled closer and she fell asleep.

When she woke again the sun was down and he was still there. "Hey, I hear you have a girlfriend."

He blushed and looked away. "No, just a friend, she—she saved my life."

"Tell me everything," Aranha said anxiously.

"Well, I attacked Quentin when he had the knife. I'm sorry I couldn't keep him from cutting you."

"It's okay, I think you helped keep him from going any deeper. I may not have been able to come back from that."

Jonah beamed a little at her praise. "Well, Quentin flung me off and I hit the wall, knocked me out for a minute. When I started to come to, I was surrounded by webmakers, they thought I was with the other wolves, I guess. They were going to kill me, I'm sure! Evelyn appeared next to me out of nowhere and told them to back off. She was glowing. I don't even think she knew how she was doing it. They stopped, with mouths hanging open and she helped me up and stayed beside me as I hurried to your side." He got quiet and a tear ran down his cheek.

"I was so scared when I saw you lying there, but Evelyn said you were going to be fine. Dag was dripping his blood into your mouth and that other webmaker was touching your stomach and speaking in a language I didn't recognize. Then Evelyn leaned down and kissed your forehead. You woke up, and now you're going to be fine, right?"

"Yeah, I am going to be fine." She was sure she was, she felt surprisingly pain free and very determined to move past all of this quickly.

"You're awake?" Dag said, coming in with a cup of something steaming. "Tea, Thekla said you must drink it whether you want to or not; so I guess, you'd better."

Aranha sat up and Jonah slipped off the bed and out of the room. To find Evelyn she assumed.

"It's nice that he isn't so glued to your side. I think he came into himself a little bit during the fight."

"Yeah, I think we might be moving toward a more healthy relationship."

Dag helped her arrange pillows behind her back and handed her the tea. It smelled like dirt. "What is it?"

"No idea, but she says if you can't feed, this is the best thing for your healing. There are a few bodies marinating around the living room, but they won't be ready for another day or two apparently."

Dag was doing a very good job of hiding his unease about that, but Aranha didn't miss it. "How are things going out there with the daywalkers and webmakers?"

"Drink your tea," he ordered gruffly and settled into a chair. "Thekla and Enya are in charge of the clan, they are strong willed and have little desire to be here, but they won't leave as long as you are ill and I've heard them talk. They want to take you, and Evelyn too."

"Oh," she wasn't sure what to say to that. She wasn't surprised, but she also knew that she didn't want to leave Dag. "Well, I don't think that's necessarily the best path."

"I think its bullshit," Dag hissed. "Aranha, I saw you die, I fed you my blood to help bring you back and I have no desire to ever let you out of my sight again." His words were fierce, but it was the look in his eyes that really convinced her. His feelings were deep and they were rooted in his soul.

She could feel her own soul crying out in answer. "Yeah, I agree, bullshit," she said quietly, her voice cracking with emotion.

He relaxed a little. "Drink the tea," he ordered again. "You need strength. I don't know if the vampires are going to come back and I want to get out of here as soon as we can."

"They weren't all killed?"

"No, some got away along with some of the werewolves. I don't know if they are going to try and reclaim this place, but it would be best if you weren't laid up in bed when it happened."

Aranha drank the tea, it wasn't good, but she managed to finish it. "Is everyone else of the opinion that the webmakers should go back where they came from?"

"No! All of the daywalkers want them to stay and a few of the webmakers have expressed a desire to stay and," he looked at her with an eyebrow raised, "have babies."

Aranha laughed. "Horny, are they?"

"Seems like they just haven't been able to find a replacement for their perfect mates," he said with glee.

Aranha rolled her eyes. "Full of yourself a bit?"

He leaned close and kissed her gently. "Don't I have reason to be?"

She smiled as he ran his tongue over her lips. "Yeah, you do."

"Did she finish her tea?" Enya said, not bothering to knock.

"She did," Dag said, grabbing the cup and handing it off to her without looking. "Now go away."

"I would, but I need to make sure my patient is well. It seems we are going to be having some company."

Dag stood up lightning quick. "What do you mean?"

"A vampire was spotted outside the fence, everyone has been called inside. We need to be prepared for an attack," Enya explained.

"How many could there be? Last night was a massacre, thanks to the webmakers," Aranha said. She spun her legs over the edge of the bed and with Dag's help, stood up surprisingly strong.

"It's impossible to know how many escaped and how many they could have called in from nearby." Dag hissed. "We never should have stayed here into the night. Dammit!"

"Like picking her up and making her travel was such a good idea," Enya hissed back, "and where would you have gone that they wouldn't have found you?"

Dag ignored her.

"Where are my weapons?" Aranha demanded, she was not going to be caught unarmed. She looked down at herself, realizing she was dressed in Dag's dress shirt from last night. "And I need pants."

"I'll bring you clothes," Enya said, hurrying off in a huff.

"Your weapons are there, but you should stay out of the way, you aren't healed."

"Dag, if this relationship is going to work, you are going to have to accept that I will *always* fight to protect those I love."

A deep guttural sound came out of his chest and he crushed her to him. "This relationship is working," he said and claimed her mouth in a deep kiss, all caution for her condition apparently gone.

She answered with enthusiasm, running her hands into his hair and pulling him closer. Their tongues caressed and their bodies began to move against each other.

"No time for that, another one was spotted," Enya said, coming into the room with a bundle of clothes. "Everyone's gathering in the entryway." She hurried back out.

"Get dressed and meet me in the entryway," Dag ordered and hurried out.

Dag left the room with a warm buzz in his body. Being around her was intoxicating. Even more so now that he'd almost lost her. Knowing that his blood had played a part in bringing her back was satisfying on a primal level and he wanted to claim her body again, very soon.

When he got to the entryway and saw his people gathered and ready for a fight, all thoughts of the bedroom emptied and his mind focused. The webmakers had positioned themselves on the stairs, looking down on the daywalkers gathered in the foyer. At the bottom of the steps stood Enya and Thekla, glaring into the placating face of Sten.

"We are not watching you fight this battle, we are warriors!" Enya was shouting.

"Women don't belong on the front lines is all I'm saying," Sten reasoned.

"You see?" Thekla said, turning to look at the women gathered behind her. "This is why we can't live in peace with these assholes. They want to contain and control us, treat us like we are something less than them."

"No, we want to cherish and protect you, so stop being a bitch and just let us," Sten hissed.

Jonah and Evelyn came up behind Dag. "This doesn't look good," Jonah whispered.

"This is not how we should be meeting an enemy," Dag said.

"No, this is why I am here," Evelyn sighed.

She stepped forward and pushed her way to the center of the arguing. Positioning herself between Enya and Sten. She held up a hand and waited for silence.

Aranha joined him and Jonah then, all eyes on Evelyn.

"Eve has something she wants me to tell you." Evelyn began softly. "She is here because she has watched her children suffer for far too long." She paused and there was no sound in the room. "She will not watch them all die tonight. We have to work together, as equals or we will forever be victims of the enemies who wish to harm us, enemies that are only our enemies because of our fear of them. She knows this and she regrets it with her entire being." She looked at Jonah. "I think we all know better now, but that doesn't change the fact that we are going to be attacked momentarily. Today we fight and tomorrow we try and make peace!" she yelled, and a cheer went up through the gathered warriors.

Dag put an arm around Aranha. "I for one, think webmakers and daywalkers belong together, so let's prove it!" Dag shouted and there was another answering yell. "Jonah, take Evelyn and lock yourselves in a closet. Nothing with windows. Don't come out until we come for you or the sun is up." He looked at the boy and sighed, he had a look of disappointment in his eyes. Dag put a hand on his shoulder. "This is not about your ability to help us fight, this is about your mission to keep Evelyn safe. She is far too young to fight and if we are worried about her, we won't be able to fight like we must. Do you understand? Can you protect her?"

"Yes, sir!" he said with a ferocity that Dag hadn't thought the boy possessed.

"Go, now," he ordered.

Jonah hugged Aranha. "Stay alive," he said quickly then found Evelyn in the crowd and pulled her away.

"Good thinking," Aranha said, pulling out a knife.

"Yeah, if I thought you'd go, I would have sent you, too."

Aranha laughed and kissed him briefly, "I know." She winked and motioned to the door. "I think it's time."

An explosion at the front door surprised them all.

CHAPTER TWENTY

Aranha crouched in a ready position as people around her scrambled to get up after being thrown from where they were. Pieces of door, wall, and window were laying all around and she had a pain in her thigh that told her she'd been hit by something. A quick touch told her it wasn't bleeding, just a bruise.

"Don't you dare die," Dag hissed.

"Been there, done that. Not going back any time soon," she responded.

There was a flurry of movement outside the new hole in the wall. It was too dark to see clearly; the attackers had taken out the floodlights and plunged the yard into darkness. They were smart, unfortunately.

"Kill the lights!" Aranha yelled, if they stayed in the light, they were at a disadvantage. Someone scrambled and hit the switch, plunging them into darkness and slowly the figures outside took shape. "Fuck," Aranha groaned.

There were at least thirty vampires standing behind a line of even more huge werewolves growling and baring their teeth.

They had come back in force to claim their place at the top of the food chain.

"Send out the girl and we will leave you all alive," A vampire called from the center of the line.

"Fuck you!" Enya called out. She'd moved to the doorway, Sten was beside her. They were presenting a united front against this enemy.

"We don't want to kill you, we would prefer to live in peace together," Sten called.

"Why would we live in peace with a subordinate species? You are no better than food for us and the fact that Quentin was willing to treat you as something else was a disgrace."

That seemed to be it, no one else spoke for a long moment, it was a stare down. Who would make the first move? Aranha wondered if Quentin had some kind of soft spot for daywalkers. More likely he was just keeping them close so he could sacrifice Lars.

A howl rippled through the werewolves and everyone moved at once. The werewolves leaped forward, vampires rushed behind them. Inside the house, daywalkers and webmakers flowed out onto the porch and yard, instinctually working as one.

"Stay close, we'll fight together," Dag said, meeting her eyes. There was trust there, he wasn't asking her to stick close so he could protect her, he was asking her to stick close so they could watch each other's backs.

Aranha smiled. "Always."

They moved through the hole in the wall and out into the battle. Metal was meeting metal all around and there were growls and hisses as immortals clashed. Blood from something somewhere splashed across Aranha's face and she didn't dare think about who's it might be. Feelings didn't belong in battle.

A werewolf flew at her from the left, claws out and teeth

bared. She crouched at the last second, reaching up and letting her knife slip into its soft belly as it continued over her. It landed with a thud at Dag's feet, dead.

"Nice," he said with a nod, then turned as a vampire came at him from the right.

Aranha spun as a vampire came at her. The vampire was fast, knocking the knife from her hand and grabbing her wrist. He pulled her close. The vampire's other hand went to Aranha's throat, squeezing slowly.

"Spider bitch," the vampire hissed and bared his fangs, venom dripped from them.

"Yeah, but I can fight," Aranha responded, grabbing another blade from her belt and lashing out. She caught the vampire in the stomach, knocking him back. Aranha didn't waste any time, she rushed forward and slashed the vampire's throat then stabbed into his heart.

The scream that the vampire let out was a gurgling noise as blood poured from his mouth and wounds. Aranha wanted to watch and appreciate the kill, but she was immediately attacked by a female vampire and this one was smart enough to keep a bit of a distance, lashing out with a long sword and stepping back out of reach of Aranha's small blade.

"You think you can take over, this isn't your place. Earth was meant for us, webmaker."

"Earth wasn't meant for anyone," she hissed back. "Nothing more than a punishment for poor decisions; but here we are, making the best of it," Aranha laughed and dipped, throwing herself at her legs. She was caught off guard, falling backward and dropping her sword. As Aranha was standing back up, ready to drive her knife into her chest, Dag was already there, punching a hole into her chest and ripping her black heart out.

"Teamwork," Dag said, pulling her in for a quick kiss. There was blood on both their faces and the taste was tantalizing.

Aranha's whole body was on fire with adrenaline. Thoughts of killing mixed with thoughts of wrestling him down to the ground in a very confusing and erotic image that made her giggle with excitement.

Dag gave her a curious look then turned to take on the next enemy that was approaching. Aranha turned to catch anything else coming their way. She looked out across the yard and was surprised to see that most of the fighting had stopped. Bodies were littered across the yard and those left standing were covered in blood, breathing heavy, and grinning with triumph.

In the end there were losses on all sides. A few of the vampires and werewolves who weren't killed, begged for mercy and left with tails tucked. Aranha and Dag were both cut and bruised but healing quickly. Sten hadn't survived and Aranha couldn't decide how she felt about that. He had been her father apparently, but he had also tried to give her out to his men to breed.

Enya and Thekla were both hurt but alive, thanks to Fiske and Calder who stood before them and beat back the enemy while they crawled to safety.

Aranha wasn't the only one who was feeling frisky after the battle, more than a few pairs of bloody and battle-weary couples were embracing in the middle of their fallen enemies, brothers, and sisters. It was a welcome sight, love and lust springing up in the middle of all this hate and bloodshed.

Jonah and Evelyn rushed out onto the porch when the yelling stopped.

"You were supposed to wait until I came for you," Dag chastised.

"It was too quiet, we weren't sure if everyone was dead," he said sheepishly, then ran over to embrace Aranha.

She petted his head and smiled down at him. "It's over. I

think we're safe, for now." She really hoped so, she hurt and she was emotionally wrecked.

The survivors settled into the living room, none talking for a while. Emotions were high and as the adrenaline left, they were all feeling the pain of loss.

"Where do we go from here?" Evelyn asked, breaking the silence.

By the look of the cuddling couples in the room, it was not as simple as going back to the way things were. Aranha knew it and she met Enya's gaze across the room. The woman looked disappointed but resigned. Aranha grabbed Dag's hand and waited expectantly.

"I think it's time that we come together as one clan. Now we are both less and if we separate again I'm afraid it will be far too easy for us to be eradicated," Enya said.

The room breathed a sigh of relief at her words, then all eyes started looking around the room for a daywalker to speak up.

"You are the daywalker leader now, Dag, I assume," Fiske said quickly.

"Why him?" Harold hissed.

"Because whoever mated with Aranha was to be crowned king. She's Sten's daughter, she's queen," Calder said fiercely.

Harold sank back in his seat, pouting.

Aranha gave Dag a curious look. "Are you my king?" she asked and couldn't help the lilt of amusement in her voice.

"I guess it's better than some of the other options," he whispered in her ear, then straightened. "I will take on the responsibility with Aranha by my side. We will happily join clans, protect each other, and try to make a new way."

Cheers went up in the room and even as they thought about all they'd lost, there was a brighter future looking ahead and they all saw that. They still had a way to go to be truly safe, but it was a journey they were going to be on together.

The next few days were busy. They had decided as a group that it would be best to move into the vampire compound because of its size and security options. Of course that meant cleaning up a lot of dead bodies both inside and out, reconstruction of the front entryway and moving of belongings from the daywalker's previous compound. The webmakers would have to make a pilgrimage back for their own belongings at some point, but didn't seem in a rush to separate from the new clan.

Jonah spent much of his time with Evelyn, and Aranha missed his closeness while at the same time, couldn't be more thankful that he was comfortable enough to branch out on his own. Dag gave him jobs to do and he was feeling more useful and a visible pride was building within him. He walked taller and when she'd seen him shift recently, his wolf was larger.

Eventually she knew Dag wanted to send Jonah out to make contact with the local werewolves, try and build an alliance with them. She feared that day, wondering if they would kill him, or if he would choose them over this clan. He was the only werewolf here and had never experienced a life with others of his kind. It might be something he couldn't avoid craving. She'd never thought she'd love being with her own kind so much. Every day she felt her strength growing and the bonds with her sisters solidifying. It was something indescribably wonderful. Would he find something similar within a wolf pack?

She knew that he had saved her as much as she'd saved him. Since that night she'd discovered him, cowering on a dirty mattress, she hadn't once questioned her right to exist, or desire to live. If it wasn't for him, she may never have stayed in the city so long, never would have found Dag. Never would have been dragged into this situation where she had found her sisters. Fate had brought them all together.

Aranha looked across the room, Evelyn was sitting and watching her as she'd been deep in thought. Aranha saw someone else flash behind Evelyn's eyes; Eve was looking out and nodding. Fate indeed had played a part in all of this. Her time to be in the garden certainly wasn't a year ago, wasn't a week ago, and wouldn't be for a long while, she hoped. Eve's eyes dipped down to Aranha's belly and Aranha sucked in a hissed breath.

"No," she whispered and clutched her stomach.

"Oh yes, the first of many to be born here," Eve said with confidence.

Evelyn blinked and came back to herself, looking briefly confused then shrugging and looking back at the book she'd been reading. Jonah walked in and sat beside Evelyn, putting a familiar arm around her. Fate had done a lot it seemed.

Aranha left the room in search of Dag, she had to tell him the good news.

MEET THE AUTHOR

Courtney Davis is an author of urban fantasy, paranormal, supernatural fiction with a little romance and humor thrown in. She loves creating worlds and exploring human, and inhuman, interaction. She lives in North Idaho with her husband and children where she teaches and enjoys time spent relaxing in the summer sun and winters by the fire. She has always had an affinity for reading and writing and a goal to make a career of it. There is no greater joy than to know her words took a reader out of reality for a time and into another world.

OTHER TITLES FROM 5 PRINCE PUBLISHING

www.5princebooks.com

A Spider in the Garden *Courtney Davis*
Megan's Choice *Darci Garcia*
Something Forbidden*Bernadette Marie*
Something Found *Bernadette Marie*
Something Discovered *Bernadette Marie*
Something Lost *Bernadette Marie*
Ashes of Aldyr *Russell Archey*
Paige Devereaux *Bernadette Marie*
Max Devereaux *Bernadette Marie*
Christmas Cookies on a Cruise Ship *Parker Fairchild*
Chase Devereaux *Bernadette Marie*
Kennedy Devereaux *Bernadette Marie*
The Seven Spires *Russell Archey*